M★A★S★H
MANIA

M★A★S★H
MANIA

★ ★ ★ ★ ★ ★ ★ ★

Richard "Hooker"

AF

DODD, MEAD & COMPANY
NEW YORK

1 2 3 4 5 6 7 8 9 10

Library of Congress Cataloging in Publication Data

Hooker, Richard.
    M*A*S*H mania.

    I. Title.
PZ4.H78Maw [PS3558.O55]   813'.5'4   77–22709
ISBN 0–396–07508–8

CONTENTS

M★A★S★H
MANIA

1

SPRUCE HARBOR
MEDICAL CENTER

THIS BOOK is about Hawkeye Pierce, Duke Forrest,
Trapper John McIntyre and Spearchucker Jones. Their
names are listed in order of their arrival at the 4077th
Mobile Army Surgical Hospital in Korea back in 1951. I
was a Medical Service Corps officer in that hospital. I
grew up in Port Waldo, Maine, where I went to high
school with Hawkeye Pierce. Hawk and I, along with Me
Lay Marston, my anesthesiologist, and Wooden Leg Wilcox, my Chairman of the Board, were classmates and
fraternity brothers at Androscoggin College.

I refer to Ezekiel Bradbury (Me Lay) Marston as "my"
anesthesiologist because I am the administrator of what
is known, now, as Spruce Harbor Medical Center. My
hospital, despite blights like its (I won't say "my") medical director, Goofus MacDuff, has been declared one of
the three best hospitals in cities with populations of less
than 50,000. I am proud to run this hospital. I am proud
of my medical staff. My leading doctors are controversial, openly disliked and constantly attacked (until their
critics need surgery) by outraged citizens and paramedical varieties because they have made a career of abusing
leading citizens and paramedical varieties. Why is it? As

1

soon as some guy in a town like Spruce Harbor becomes a leading citizen, he wants to run the hospital or anyway be on the board of directors. Paramedical varieties, who always feel unfulfilled, include psychologists. A "medical center" has to have a Mental Health Clinic. Therefore psychologists. A psychologist is defined by Hawkeye Pierce as a blivot. A blivot, he says, is two hundred pounds of wet manure in a hundred-pound bag.

I believe that I have the best staff of physicians in a comparable hospital anywhere, certainly in Maine. There are family physicians on my staff, like Doggy Moore, but no one in my hospital does a damn thing in the specialty areas unless he is a certified specialist. My Chairman of the Board, Mr. Wooden Leg Wilcox, does what I, and my doctors, tell him, most of the time. Wooden Leg has a Board that does what he tells it. The Spruce Harbor Medical Center may not run like a Swiss clock, but as we say hereabouts, "it runs some good." I, most of my staff and my Chairman of the Board figure that our job is to serve the public. We know that the only way to do this is to have a highly trained, dedicated staff and an illiterate Board of Directors.

"I don't want nobody on this Board can read or write too good," my Chairman frequently proclaims. So far the quality of our product and the fact that the hospital breaks even financially has kept the community wolves at bay. It's said that an honest hospital must lose money. This is true, but our situation is a little different. Wooden Leg Wilcox is not only Chairman of the Board. He is the owner of the Finestkind Fish Market and the Finestkind Lobster Pound, which share Harbor Point with the hospital, the Finestkind Clinic and the Penobscot Mental Health Clinic.

"Wooden Leg," I said to my Chairman a couple years back, "how come the hospital finances seem so obscure, even to me, most of the time? How come one week I can barely meet the payroll and a month later we're showing a profit?"

"I gotta buy lobsters, ain't I? Hey look, boy. Don't sweat it. I need cash to buy everything around when the price is down, so I grab a little out of the hospital. Then when the price is right I unload. You make a little, I make a little. Don't I deserve something?"

"Wooden Leg," I said, "you're a thief!"

"I was a thief, this joint'd have to close up. So I put a little Blue Cross dough into lobsters, maybe a trip of nice haddock. Ain't that better'n beggin' from the government? I need working capital and the hospital gets most of the profit."

The hospital, clinics and Wooden Leg's fish complex occupy Harbor Point about a mile from the center of town. The setting, with its view of Penobscot Bay and the Camden Hills, makes Spruce Harbor Medical Center an unusually pleasant place in which to get well or to die. A pleasant place to work, too. I'm the only hospital administrator in Maine who can relax, do my job, and do it efficiently. Of course, I do have problems. When I have them, they tend to differ from those of many, perhaps all, other hospital administrators. Most of my problems are ridiculous, often created by what some consider the eccentricity of my surgical staff. An example was my trouble last summer with the MCRL (that's the Maine Civil Rights League).

I'd like to explain something here and now because so much of this book, directly or indirectly, expresses the opinions and documents the habits and contrariness of

3

my chief surgeon, Dr. Hawkeye Pierce. Hawkeye spent most of his life in or around Spruce Harbor, where we have a variety of ethnic groups, and has chosen, as his nonmedical associates, citizens from what a local intellectual calls the rough-and-tumble element of our society. He has adopted and maybe enlarged upon the speech habits of this element. He often refers to blacks as niggers or coons, to French Canadians as frogs and lily pad jumpers and swamp canaries, to Italians as guineas, to Lebanese as camel drivers, to Jews as Hebes. Therefore he is automatically branded a bigot by certain people. "These folks are interesting," Hawk says. "They hear a colloquial ethnic designation and they have an alarm reaction. They think that the words automatically degrade the individual. They don't understand that under certain circumstances these same words establish a bond of understanding and even affection or, for chrissake, that half the people here or anywhere else don't know that colloquial ethnic designations are a departure from what the effete snobs consider proper."

There are about a hundred blacks in Spruce Harbor. A newly arrived physician asked Dr. Pierce a few years ago why he did nearly all the surgery on the black population.

"Because I don't keep them waiting in my office or stiff them on weekends any more than I do anybody else. They know I want to get paid if they've got it but will work for zip if I have to. They know they ain't getting no reverse Tom action from Hawkeye Pierce. Also, as I told the Reverend Johnson after I grabbed his gallbladder, you make a hole in a nigger, even a nigger preacher, you can't tell him from anybody else."

In all of Maine we have about one thousand blacks, a

4

couple thousand Indians and four thousand members (says Hawkeye Pierce) of the MCRL. Dr. Pierce believes that these four thousand include two thousand two hundred fifty Bad Hairs. A Bad Hair is anyone whose haircut extends beyond Hawkeye's crew cut. Most of the Bad Hairs are in college either as students or faculty. "The average Bad Hair," according to Hawk, "will never make as much money as any jig on a Detroit assembly line. His idea of how to bestow Civil Rights is to blow pot with the campus blacks. They're a bunch of jerks who cultivate the blacks because they hope the black cats are losing as bad as they are. They don't want to liberate the blacks. They just want to patronize them."

And then, according to Hawkeye, there are, in the MCRL, 1747 Confused Wool. Ever since Hawkeye read *Semi-Tough* by Dan Jenkins, he's been using that word "wool." This Confused Wool, he says, is about evenly divided between well-meaning but dumb Jesus Wool and Educated Wool. The Jesus Wool, like the Church of the Supreme Spirit, wouldn't know a nigger from an Armenian but would invite either to sit down and have some beans if he blew in on Saturday night. The Educated Wool is married to executives in toilet paper factories and power companies, and they've been to college, and their husbands' bosses say the broads gotta get involved, so they join the MCRL, and if they saw a nigger in the pool they'd drain it and start over.

"That's 3997. What about the other three members?" Pierce is frequently asked.

"Oh, well, nothing is 100 percent. There have to be three guys who understand what problems exist and who want to help. In Maine it's not so much racial as general. The Indians need help, but so do thousands of others. If the blacks are a problem, it's because if you put the thousand of them up against any thousand randomly selected Maine whites, the blacks come out ahead."

My trouble with the MCRL began when Spearchucker Jones sank a fifty-foot eagle putt on the 18th hole to win the Spruce Harbor Country Club championship from Hawkeye Pierce. We have a new TV station here but not much news, so the last hole was on the sports show that night. Actually, since Jones is a former all-pro fullback, I suppose this was a newsworthy event. Unfortunately, after following the putt into the hole, the camera focused on Dr. Pierce to catch his reaction. First there was a look of incredulous dismay followed by the exclamation, "Why you unconscious nigger bastard!"

Well, of course they cut out the sound, but all four thousand members of the MCRL are lip readers. This was a slow spell for infringements on civil rights. Apparently nobody's denied living space, or said an unkind word to anybody—black, red or white—for nigh on six weeks. The MCRL, restive from inactivity, mobilized. Had Spiro Agnew desecrated the grave of Martin Luther King, the heat of indignation could not have been more intense, except, as Dr. Pierce pointed out, with one thousand Confused Wool who'd never heard of Dr. King. Also, Pierce says, "There were six unconcerned Confused Wool at the Body of Jesus Tabernacle in Tedium Cove who were saving a pregnant girl. They were saving her by exorcising the devil out of her. That's religious talk for beating her up. She had two broken arms, two black eyes and bruises all over her body."

The hue and cry from everywhere persisted for several days. Dr. Oliver Wendell (Spearchucker) Jones, interviewed on Spruce Harbor TV, offered the opinion that Dr. Pierce was "a bigoted racist honkie." The interviewer, the same gentleman who, on the sports, calls the Giants' leading pitcher Jew-Ann Marichal, didn't realize what Spearchucker had said till someone told him, and then he wasn't sure he understood it.

The only voice raised in defense of Hawkeye Pierce was that of Gus Blue, the new black basketball coach at Spruce Harbor High. Gus, asked by the sports editor of the Spruce Harbor *Gazette* what he thought of Dr. Jones's fifty-foot putt, stated, "That unconscious nigger bastard couldn't sink that putt again in a million years."

There were demands that Dr. Pierce be suspended from the hospital staff. There were demands that he apologize publicly to Dr. Jones. A supercommittee of Bad Hairs and Confused Wool, headed by the Reverend Aaron (Buddy) Hamilton (Buddy hates only Catholics and booze and *Jesus Christ, Superstar*) tried to interview Dr. Pierce, whose harassed secretary finally appealed, "Hawkeye, I've got to tell them something. They demand some kind of an answer!"

"Give them an evasive answer," counseled the surgeon. "Invite them to a snipe hunt."

Finally I had to intervene and told both Hawkeye and Spearchucker that enough was enough. They'd have to do something. I was relieved and somewhat surprised when they agreed to meet the Reverend Hamilton and his committee two mornings hence, at ten o'clock, in my office. I should have known better. The two surgeons were already there when I arrived, my secretary having let them in. They were drinking my coffee and intermittently laughing and talking. Hawkeye had an old bull whip he'd resurrected from his father's barn, and he was saying, between giggles, "Chucker, if you time it right,

7

let them get a look at the scene, that Christer will probably get up and stand in your way and you can take him out like he was a pygmy linebacker."

"What are you two up to?" I demanded, knowing full well that it was a dumb question.

"Step aside, Hook," warned Hawkeye, "I'm gonna start educatin' this nigger."

Dr. Jones stepped two paces into the hall. As the Reverend Hamilton rose to greet him, Hawkeye appeared with the whip saying, "I'll teach you, Jones."

Spearchucker yelled, "Oh, heh, man," and charged down the hallway toward the front entrance with Hawkeye swinging the whip at his heels. In passing the super-committee, Chucker demonstrated to the Reverend Hamilton why he'd been an all-pro fullback.

Waiting outside in the Jones family's station wagon, loaded with golf clubs and camping gear, were Evelyn Jones and Mary Pierce. The surgeons jumped in. "Drive," Dr. Jones ordered his wife. "Fast. Get us out of here."

Drive they did, all the way to the golf course at Ingonish Beach, Nova Scotia, one of the finest anywhere. For seven hundred miles the surgeons drank beer, laughed and listened to dire threats from their wives, who claimed they'd face ostracism and social destruction upon their return.

Well, incidents like this blow over. By the time Hawk and the Chucker got back from Nova Scotia, the Bad Hairs and the Confused Wool were abusing the Republican gubernatorial aspirant, State Senator Crazy Horse Weinstein, for selling clothes to the Indians at 50 percent of the wholesale price. The Bad Hairs and the Confused Wool were split down the middle on this one. Some of

8

them claimed Crazy Horse was insulting his mother's tribesmen by offering charity, and others claimed he was a cheap Hebe for not giving the clothes for nothing. This got to be an issue in the state legislature, which debated it for days. In logical sequence, this led to an intensity of civil rights interest amongst Educated Wool wed to paper and power company executives. Their husbands told them, "The longer these rubes argue about Crazy Horse selling half-price clothes to the Indians, the less time they'll have to think up ways to put us out of business. Keep it going, honey."

My greatest problem as administrator of Spruce Harbor Medical Center, and it's chronic and recurrent, is the Penobscot Mental Health Clinic. Some of my staff, as well as my Board Chairman, are critical of its performance and go so far as to question its reason to exist. I recently received this letter from Dr. Hawkeye Pierce, who was disturbed about an incident which had occurred while he was covering the Emergency Room.

Dear Hook:

I'm increasingly annoyed, both at the absurdity of my having to cover *your* Emergency Room and at that ridiculous jerk, Rex Eatapuss, and his gaggle of useless psychologists.

There has been an insurrection of staff members who claim that they are incompetent to cover the Emergency Room. I applied for membership in this group but was rejected on the grounds that I am competent.

I offer, in rebuttal, a case history. On Saturday, November 6th, I was on Emergency Room duty. At approximately seven P.M., I was called and told that a 17-year-old boy had been brought in by his parents because he was nervous. It seemed that he'd been out in the family barn, participating in the milking of cows, when "something came over him."

"He should learn to step back," I said. "You go for that milk

9

pail any way but from the cow's right rear, surer'n hell something may come over you. Give him a bath."

"No," said the nurse, "it's not that. It seems he got very nervous. He's been seen in the Mental Health Clinic."

"Well, hell," I said, "why don't you call one of them mental healthers if they've already seen this guy. As a thoracic surgeon I am ill at ease with nervous youths of the countryside."

"We did," the nurse replied, "but they are busy coloring."

"What they hell do you mean, they are busy coloring?" I asked.

"All I know is what I was told," the nurse said brusquely. Obviously she was annoyed with me.

I'll digress here. Later investigation revealed that the mental healthers could not respond to this call because they were devoting the weekend to painting psychedelic colors on two thousand paper ducks they'd spent two weeks cutting out of Mental Health Clinic stationery. The background of this is interesting. Mr. Spiro Agnew, in a speech before the American Psychiatric Association on October 15th, said, "Show me a psychologist and I'll show you a man who's softer than the back half of a duck."

The psychologists, heretofore uncertain where they stood with Mr. Agnew and overcome by this burst of recognition, felt that Mr. Agnew's statement was a harbinger of continued and increased federal subsidization of their programs. Understandably, they could not abandon their Saturday night project for a nervous youth of the countryside.

Nervously, I went to the Emergency Room, where I met the patient. He had long, greasy, shoulder length, black hair, a black leather jacket, snug Levis, black socks and black loafers with brown around the edges. (If he'd had white socks, I'd have figured him for a $7,500/year employee of the Department of Health and Welfare.) His facial expression suggested a lack of what the shrinks used to call "affect."

The first principle in handling this sort of situation is to get everybody out of the room and establish rapport with the patient. Even a thoracic surgeon knows this. Therefore I or-

10

dered parents and nurses out and asked the sufferer, "What ails you?"

"I don't know," he said.

"You been taking drugs?" I asked. This was because I've read about kids taking drugs.

"No," he said, "I guess I'm just mixed up."

"Hey, buddy," I said, "you think you're mixed up. How'd you like to hear my life story?"

"Huh?" he said.

"You know what I think?" I asked.

He looked at me vacuously and did not respond.

"I think," I continued, "you either been thumping your dill too much or not enough."

"Huh?" he said.

"Okay, boy," I said, "I've blown the only mental health shot I got. If you want to go home, okay. If you're really upset, I'll put you in the fool farm. You call it."

"I wanta go home," said the patient.

Later I talked to the parents who asked about a psychiatrist. "Look, folks," I said, "if I knew where to find one on Saturday night I'd pay him a C-note to say I'm incompetent to cover this Emergency Room, so you can see how much help you're going to get from me."

If it wasn't like this, it was pretty damn close.

> Very truly yours,
> Benjamin F. Pierce, M.D.

Obviously, Dr. Pierce is given to exaggeration, perhaps even flights of fancy. I must hasten to explain that the distinguished head of our Mental Health Clinic is not really named Dr. Rex Eatapuss. His real name is Ferenc Ovari, M.S., Ph.D., plus this and that more after his name —degrees from Budapest, Vienna and London. Records confirming this were lost during World War II, but I have investigated his credentials thoroughly enough to

11

repudiate Pierce's contention that he's a hunky out of Scranton, Pennsylvania.

Dr. Ovari came to Spruce Harbor when our Mental Health Clinic opened in 1961. To be honest, I'm not sure how he's survived. He has created problems. The occasional psychiatrists who've set up shop here have left after, at the most, two years, citing Dr. Ovari as the reason for their departure. Therefore we've never had effective psychiatric coverage, and it's been one of our glaring defects. Why Pierce, the other surgeons, Wooden Leg Wilcox and I haven't run him off instead of just abusing him I'm not sure. Lately I've been getting vibrations about the why of it, but I'm afraid of them. One reason, I suppose, is that bugging Goofus MacDuff, the Medical Director, ceased to be fun years ago. Up to a point they tolerate Dr. Ovari for the fun of harassing him.

Dr. Ovari, despite his lack of popularity with the medical profession, and despite what I must conclude is an inability to come to grips with the mental health problem in this area, is impressive. He is now in his middle fifties and of middle height, goateed and moustached, suave, assured, disdainful of the peasants who plague him. With his accent, which has a lilt of middle Europe, he is a devastatingly effective public speaker, PR man and fund raiser. To quote our Chairman of the Board: "That jeezly Rex Eatapuss talks to my wife and the other talent at the PTA and they all come home and tell about he trained with Sigmund Freud, which he didn't even say, and they don't know if Siggy was a queer Austrian or the Patriots' number three draft choice, but they think Rex is some wonderful."

It was at a Rotary Club meeting, back in 1961, that

Wooden Leg Wilcox changed Dr. Ferenc Ovari's name to Rex Eatapuss. The Rotary Club (Hawkeye Pierce says anybody who'd join the Rotary Club would eat a wet chicken) always invites newly arrived specialists to speak. The members seldom care what the speaker has to say; nor could they understand it if they cared. On this occasion Dr. Ovari entertained his unenthralled audience with a discussion of the libidinal feelings that a child of three to six years develops toward the parent of the opposite sex. This, he told them, is called the Oedipus Complex and refers to the hero of Greek legend who murdered his father and married his mother.

The usual apathy and torpor of a Rotarian audience was shattered this time by Jocko Allcock, a business associate of Wooden Leg's, who, very juiced, recoiled in horror and disgust at this incestuous tale.

"No good Greek mother——" he started to exclaim. In midexclamation he was interrupted by Demosthenes Rock, owner of the Parthenon Motel, two miles east on Route One. Demosthenes had missed the Oedipus bit, but he'd heard Jocko's response. Since he and Jocko are frequently at odds, Demosthenes assumed that Jocko was, once again, launching a campaign of personal vilification.

Mr. Rock was temporarily restrained, but after Dr. Ovari's talk he spoke quite heatedly to Mr. Allcock. Jocko explained that his four-syllable reference had not been to Mr. Rock but "to that there Greek guy, King Eatapuss. He married his mother."

This exchange of ideas between Mr. Rock and Mr. Allcock was discussed for days in the inner sanctums of Spruce Harbor where Rotarians work and play. The outcome was inevitable. Someone, probably Wooden Leg

Wilcox, decided to perpetuate the memory of that fine meeting by changing Dr. Ovari's name to Dr. Rex Eatapuss. And so he is known, far and wide. Anyway from Damariscotta to Belfast.

"Really too bad," I said to Hawkeye Pierce soon after this episode. "Dr. Ovari is a distinguished man in his field. With his training in Vienna and . . ."

"Vienna, my ass," exclaimed the dirty-mouthed surgeon. "That hunky probably flunked out of Slippery Rock State Teachers and anointed himself with a Ph.D."

So it is that if anything interesting happens at Spruce Harbor Medical Center, you can bet that my four crazy surgeons or my controversial head psychologist are involved—usually both.

2

THE MIRACLE OF
HARBOR POINT

For three days the street in front of Dr. Spearchucker Jones's big white colonial home on Harbor Point had been lined with cars. Tweedy middle-aged females and males with baggy pants, all carrying binoculars and cameras, milled around on Dr. Jones's front lawn.

The reason for this was quite simple, but Dr. Jones's surgical colleagues, Hawkeye Pierce, Duke Forrest and Trapper John McIntyre, had not heard the word. This threesome lives somewhat apart from the mainstream of life in Spruce Harbor, Maine. It is not true, as rumored, that they think Eisenhower is still president, but they seem quite immune to news that doesn't directly concern them. They seldom get any because they never talk to anyone except each other if they can possibly avoid it.

So it was that on the third day of the Miracle of Harbor Point Hawkeye asked, "Hey, Spearchucker, what the hell's going on down your way?"

"Well, I'm pretty well known—prominent neurosurgeon, famous ex-football player and so forth. Probably all these people are just trying to catch a glimpse of me."

Doctors Pierce, Forrest and McIntyre considered this explanation briefly before their spokesman, Dr. Pierce, replied, "Quite likely. Ain't many like you in the neighborhood."

"Hey, old buddy," said Duke Forrest, "y'all need any help, just let us know."

"All you guys ever get me into is trouble. You've never gotten me out of any."

"Ingrate," stated Dr. Pierce.

This conversation was taking place in the coffee shop of the Spruce Harbor General Hospital on a Saturday morning. Trapper John sensed that the time was ripe, once again, to give the citizens of Spruce Harbor something to gossip about. Therefore he said, "Racist."

Dr. Jones picked up Trapper John, held him three feet off the floor and said, "Dr. McIntyre, I'm sure you won't object to my having lunch with your wife."

Dr. Jones waited patiently while his victim pondered the request and consulted with Hawkeye and Duke: "What does one say," Trapper asked, "when a six foot three inch, two hundred and thirty pound buck nigger asks to lunch with one's wife, and holds one up in the air while one formulates one's reply?"

"Yes, sir," Duke told him.

"Oh, yes," agreed Hawkeye. "You say, 'Yes, sir.'"

"Lemme down," begged Trapper. "I'll call her."

Dr. Jones, releasing him, announced haughtily, "It's already arranged. I'm meeting her at the Bay View in half an hour."

There was nothing unusual about this. Mrs. McIntyre, the former Lucinda Lively, and Spearchucker Jones had been close friends for years. On this particular day they were meeting to discuss Spearchucker's debut as a thespian. Lucinda is a bright light in the Spruce Harbor Players and had convinced the neurosurgeon that he should play the lead in her forthcoming production of Othello.

After their rounds, Hawkeye, Duke and Trapper decided that the November day was too cold for golf. They didn't know what to do with themselves, but as they stood in the doctors' parking lot and looked toward Harbor Point, they discovered that the crowd at Spearchucker's house was larger than ever. Needing to satisfy their curiosity, they boarded Hawkeye's station wagon and drove to where the action was. There wasn't much. The tweedies and the baggy pantsers were quietly standing in Spearchucker's yard, and at ten-minute intervals about a dozen of them went into the house. They came out with expressions of fulfillment which suggested that, at the very least, they had witnessed a miracle.

The surgeons learned little by wandering through the crowd. Trapper finally asked a little old lady what was going on and reported that, if he'd understood correctly, they'd come to see a "black-headed grossberg."

"What the hell is a black-headed grossberg?" asked Duke.

"Maybe it's a new name for a nigger," said Trapper.

"Maybe they think Spearchucker is Jewish," suggested Hawkeye.

Duke, apparently convinced that this was the case, stood up on a stone wall that separates Spearchucker's yard from the street and proclaimed, "Hey, y'all. Y'all hear this. Y'all mistaken. Dr. Jones is a Baptist."

This proclamation was received with total noncomprehension by the crowd, which obviously wanted no one to intrude upon their bliss, whether already realized or anticipated. Mrs. Evelyn Jones observed the performance and sent her sixteen-year-old son, Oliver Wendell

17

Jones, Jr., with a message for Duke. "Uncle Duke," he said, "my mama says if you guys don't clear out, I gotta take you apart."

"Come on, Duke," yelled Hawkeye. "Even Spearchucker's scared of that cat. Let's have lunch."

Meanwhile Trapper approached another pilgrim, a white-haired gentleman clad in knickers and a Sherlock Holmes hat, saying, "Hey, Pop, the coon is at the Bay View. Spread the word."

"I beg your pardon?"

"The jungle bunny. He's having lunch with my wife at the Bay View. You wanta help me get him?"

As the station wagon sped toward the Bay View, leaving the pilgrims in confusion, Mrs. Jones mingled with them and calmed their fears by explaining that the three interlopers were crazy. At the Bay View the surgeons found Spearchucker and Lucinda McIntyre laughing over a drink while Spearchucker described the coffee shop episode.

"What you up to, Chucker?" demanded Duke. "You growin' watermelons in your cellar?"

"If you guys can't think up some new ones," answered the large neurosurgeon, "why don't you pick on Angelo for a while?"

Angelo, the bartender, overheard and protested, "Forget it. These guys ain't had a new guinea joke in five years."

"You can't sit with us," Lucinda declared. "We have important things to discuss."

"You think that big stove lid's another Paul Robeson?" Hawkeye asked Lucinda. "He don't even know the tune to 'We Shall Overcome'!"

Forced to eat alone, the surgeons ordered drinks and

interrogated Angelo. "You seen any black-headed gross-bergs around?" asked Hawkeye.

"What I don't know is how come I let everyone in my family get operated on by you guys," Angelo answered evasively.

"Maybe it's because you're stupid," suggested Trapper John.

"That occurred to me," agreed Angelo. "You want another mart?"

At this point Duke insisted, "I wanta know what is a black-headed grossberg."

The answer came from a large dark-skinned hawk-nosed gentleman who, uninvited but welcome, settled into the fourth seat at the surgeons' table.

"Pheucticus melanocephalus," said State Senator Solomon (Crazy Horse) Weinstein in answer to Duke's question. In 1920 Crazy Horse's father, an itinerant peddler, had married Marcia Running Tide, a full-blooded Passamaquoddy Indian girl. In 1971 Crazy Horse wanted to be governor and owned the five best gents furnishing stores in the State of Maine.

"All one needs do," said Hawkeye, "is sit in the Bay View and the world comes a-callin'. Welcome, Crazy Horse."

"What was that you said?" demanded Duke.

"Pheucticus melanocephalus."

"They had them Israeli-Injun studies after I left school. What the hell's that mean?" asked Hawkeye.

"A black-headed grosbeak. A bird. A bird that belongs out in Saskatchewan and British Columbia has come to roost in Spruce Harbor, Maine, in Spearchucker's back yard. Mrs. Jones identified him and notified the Audubon Society. Bird-watchers from all over New England have

19

come to see the black-headed grosbeak."

Hawkeye was obviously struggling to grasp the meaning, the significance, of this revelation. He just didn't seem able to make it.

"How big is this bird?" asked Duke.

"He might run five to seven inches, stem to stern," Crazy Horse told him.

"There was a great dogfight on the hospital lawn three days ago," said Hawkeye, "but it bombed. Didn't draw more than half a dozen. But a six-inch bird packs them in."

Probably the surgeons would have forgotten all about the black-headed grosbeak had there not been a cocktail party and dinner that night at the home of Dr. Ezekiel Bradbury (Me Lay) Marston, the Spruce Harbor anesthesiologist. Me Lay's wife, Charlotte, is somewhat socially inclined. She's so socially inclined that her parties are command performances that even Doctors Pierce, Forrest and McIntyre attend with their wives. The surgeons, forced to try to behave like pillars of the community, nearly always fortify themselves in advance, and this night was no exception. Dr. and Mrs. Spearchucker Jones, of course, were there. Mrs. Jones was giddy with delight over the bird situation, but, early on, Dr. Jones indicated to his colleagues that he was beginning to tire of bird-watchers.

As usual, the four surgeons wound up in one corner of their host's bar and playroom along with Crazy Horse Weinstein and Wooden Leg Wilcox, the business manager of the Finestkind Clinic and Fish Market. The conversation turned to birds. Spearchucker, as time passed, became increasingly sure that, despite his devotion to wildlife and the ecology in general, he wanted peace and quiet at home.

Dinner was served—a walkabout dinner—but, despite occasional forays into the eye of the social whirl, the corner group stayed quite tight. At 9:30 Crazy Horse Weinstein announced, "I got a bird suit down at the store. Some clown I met at a buyer's thing in New York sent it to me. Bird's head, beak, wings, everything. Need a big guy to fill it out."

"You lay upon me the kernel of an idea, Crazy Horse," mused Spearchucker Jones. "A black-headed grosbeak has orange underparts, a black head and white wing patches. Could your bird suit be altered to these specifications?"

"Easy," said Crazy Horse, who is not called Crazy Horse just because of his aboriginal background. "Just what do you have in mind, Spearchucker?"

"Well, it seems to me that maybe we oughta have two black-headed grosbeaks. If one of them went about four ounces and the other over two hundred pounds, either these nuts would go away and leave me alone or I'd draw thousands and be able to sell season tickets at fifty bucks apiece."

"Excellent thinking," agreed Hawkeye, "although two-hundred-pound black-headed grosbeaks are tough to find."

"The bird suit would just about fit you, Hawk," said Crazy Horse.

"No way," protested Hawkeye. "I ain't wearin' no bird suit. You think I'm strange?"

"Strange you should ask," commented Trapper John. "Maybe we could get Halfaman Timberlake. He's sort of birdlike."

The group felt this suggestion had obvious merit. Halfaman, although a trifle slow mentally, is an invaluable employee of Wooden Leg Wilcox and his partner in many business ventures, Mr. Jocko Allcock. Halfaman weighs around two hundred pounds, and everyone decided that he'd make a great black-headed grosbeak.

State Senator Crazy Horse Weinstein, whose career in business and politics has been characterized by his ability to act decisively and effectively, said, "Okay, I'll go down to the store and fix up that bird suit. I'll meet you guys at Bette Bang Bang's joint in an hour. Be there. Halfaman's bound to be, but I don't want to show up alone at a whorehouse with a bird suit."

"Why not?" asked Hawk. "If we got some pictures, it might do wonders for your gubernatorial aspirations."

"We'll be there, Horse," Spearchucker assured him, "and without photographers. You are a true friend."

Bette Bang Bang, Mattress Mary and Made Marion have been in business for some fifteen years down on Elm Street. Prostitution is not legal in Maine, but neither is it defined in such a way that whatever authorities exist have seriously tried to curtail the Elm Street effort. This is partly because Dr. Doggy Moore, Spruce Harbor's leading all-around messiah, physician and Maine Senior Golf Champion, has taken care of the girls and proclaimed that their whorehouse solves more problems than it creates. Dr. Moore has kept the VD rate in Spruce Harbor lower than any other town in Maine. Twice weekly at 4:30 P.M., Doggy examines the girls and takes smears and cultures. On the wall of his inner office is a plaque bestowed upon him by his surgical friends. The plaque reads:

Between the dark and the daylight,
When the night begins to lower,
Comes a crisis in the day's occupation
Which is known as the prostitutes' hour.

Dr. Moore is pleased with this. Ninety percent of his patients can't read well enough to dig it. With the other 10 percent, it becomes a conversation piece and adds to the legend of Doggy Moore.

In 1969, Bette Bang Bang, because the economy was burgeoning and because she, Mattress Mary and Made Marion were getting a mite tired, took on three new girls. Their real names, if they have any, are unknown, so Doggy Moore named them Graveyard Alice, Infected Allegra, and Edie with the Great Big Pair. They are named quite inappropriately after grave Alice and laughing Allegra and Edith with golden hair, the heroines of Longfellow's poem paraphrased on Doggy's plaque.*

Of the three, Graveyard Alice, a six-foot, one-hundred-and-seventy-pound redhead, is outstanding. In her two years there on the job, two of her customers, clearly overmatched, have suffered fatal myocardial infarctions while partaking of her favors. An enterprising local funeral director offered, for five bucks, flight insurance to each of Alice's customers. He guaranteed complete, discreet saddle-to-the-grave service to any subscriber who felt that, should all not go well, his image might be tarnished by cooling out in a whorehouse. This, plus Doggy

---

*In addition to the original manuscript of *MASH* by Richard Hooker, the works of Mr. Longfellow, a nineteenth-century poet and writer, are on display in the Androscoggin College library.

Moore's statement that twenty minutes with Alice is the equivalent, in exercise, to jogging three miles and a helluva lot more fun, has made her a busy girl.

At ten forty-five the four surgeons left the party to keep the rendezvous on Elm Street. Crazy Horse, with bird suit, waited patiently in his Eldorado a cautious fifty yards east of the whorehouse. Bette Bang Bang was a trifle disconcerted when five such prominent citizens, none of them a customer, and one of them with a bird suit, crossed her threshold. Addressing Hawkeye, she exclaimed, "What the hell do you guys want?"

"Be easy, Bette," Hawkeye said soothingly. "We just wanta see Halfaman. We got a new suit for him."

Crazy Horse Weinstein held up the bird suit.

"What the christ kind of a suit izzat?" demanded Bette.

"Vassar?" asked Trapper.

"No, I believe Bette was Wellesley," said Hawkeye, who explained. "Latest thing from Brooks Brothers, Bette. Just right for Halfaman. It's kind of like a bird suit."

Bette Bang Bang, sensing that she might be in over her depth, sighed and said, "Halfaman's in the kitchen, restin' up for Alice. He goes on in fifteen minutes."

The group moved to the kitchen where Halfaman Timberlake, graying, handsome, horny, happy and normally somewhat confused, was drinking beer and staring vacantly at a TV set. "How they goin', Halfaman?" Hawkeye asked.

"Oh, hi, Hawk."

"We got a job for you, Halfaman," said Spearchucker, "and we got a new suit for you. We'll give you the suit if you'll wear it in my back yard tomorrow morning."

24

It figures that the average guy, presented with a bird suit by Crazy Horse Weinstein, would categorically reject it. Halfaman is not the average guy. He put on the suit, flapped his wings and babbled, more or less incoherently, with what seemed to be pleasure.

"Halfaman learns quick," observed Duke. "He even talks like a bird."

"We gotta have a trial run," Hawkeye declared. "We gotta find out whether he seems authentic. We can't just send him cold into Chucker's back yard without practice. After all, they're pro bird-watchers. They'll spot a phony in a second."

"Okay," said Crazy Horse. "Let him try it out on Graveyard Alice. If she responds, maybe the bird-watchers will."

Halfaman was warming to his role and becoming more and more excited as his date with Graveyard Alice approached. Bette Bang Bang, entering the kitchen to give Halfaman the two-minute alert, saw him hopping like a bird, flapping his wings like a bird and looking pretty much like a bird.

"Sweet Jesus," exclaimed Bette. "You ain't gonna send him to Alice like that? He'll scare her to death."

"What's wrong with a nice clean bird after some of your regular customers?" demanded Hawkeye, who turned to the bird and said, "Hop to it, Halfaman."

Trapper John McIntyre, basically a philosopher and aware of current trends, said to the group, "Surely with all the government subsidized research on human behavior, there must have been papers written about this sort of situation. Perhaps before sending a guy in a bird suit into a prostitute's room we should have read up on it."

Turning to Bette Bang Bang, Duke said, "Hey, Bette, get the latest *Quarterly Cumulative Medical Index* and look up 'Bird suits; effect on prostitutes.'"

"Huh?"

"It might be under 'Prostitutes; reaction to bird suits,'" said Hawkeye.

"Of course," said Trapper, "this may be a variant that has escaped Big Brother."

"When you come right down to it, and regardless of scientific research," observed Crazy Horse Weinstein, "you don't have to be too smart to figure that any broad, even Graveyard Alice, is going to react negatively to Halfaman Timberlake in a bird suit."

If Crazy Horse had presented this theory to the proper authorities, he might have received fifty G's over a two-year period to prove it. No amount of research, however, could have added to the Weinstein theory, which was confirmed immediately by Graveyard Alice. She ran naked from her room screaming, "It's a big bird. A big sonovabitch of a bird."

"You're right, Alice," Hawkeye assured her. "Daddy was a whippoorwill and mommy was a Saint Bernard."

"That's no ordinary bird, honey," explained Spear-chucker Jones. "That's a black-headed grosbeak and he came all the way from Saskatchewan to meet you."

Alice, suddenly aware of her nakedness, covered herself with a bathrobe which Bette Bang Bang gave her. "I don't care where he came from," Alice protested. "I ain't takin' care of no bird."

"Would you say, Alice," asked Trapper, "that you are ecologically oriented?"

"What the hell are you talkin' about?"

"It's very simple, Alice," explained Hawkeye. "This is

a very rare bird, and he's a very horny bird. The bird book says a black-headed grosbeak's gotta make love once a week or his feathers fall off. You wouldn't want that to happen, would you?"

Graveyard Alice, indicating no ecological orientation, said, "I don't care if his feathers fall off. I ain't servicin' no bird."

While this dialogue progressed in the hallway, Halfaman, The Greatest Black-Headed Grosbeak of Them All, his love unrequited, hopped and flew out of Alice's room and tried other rooms. Three rooms away, where Edie with the Great Big Pair was pacifying Jocko Allcock, Halfaman discovered that the door was not locked. He hopped in, flapping his wings. In a falsetto voice with undertones of bass, he stated, "Peep, peep."

Jocko, normally a cool head and usually privy to all that was going on, had not been involved in this action. In panic, he raced for the door and charged down the hall toward the bird discussion group, where Graveyard Alice, despite the blandishments of the surgeons, still was expressing her disinclination to enter into any business agreement, regardless of price, with a bird, however rare, however great his need.

"Evenin', Jocko," said Hawkeye to the late arrival who stopped, confused and naked, in midflight and babbled incoherently in a language which, to the trained ear, sounded like gutter invective. "What seems to be your major maladjustment?"

"I hope y'all ain't changed over, Jocko," said Duke. "Ain't none of us here interested, but if we were, your credential would be impressive, even in its obviously obtunded state."

Mr. Jocko Allcock's possible response was interrupted

27

by The Greatest Grosbeak who joined the group and stated once more, "Peep, peep." At this point Dr. Spearchucker Jones decided that Halfaman's grosbeak credibility had been conclusively established. "Okay, folks," he said, "Halfaman has passed the test. You come to my house tomorrow morning at eleven o'clock, Halfaman, with your new suit. Pleasant evening, everybody. We must get back to our party."

Jocko and Alice and Edie were somewhat put out, but forgave all when the situation was explained to them. Graveyard Alice insisted on taking care of Halfaman, bird suit and all, and later proclaimed that "birds ain't bad."

Dr. Spearchucker Jones has a swimming pool in his back yard and, behind it, a pool house. At 11:15 on Sunday morning, The Greatest Black-Headed Grosbeak suddenly appeared on the roof of the pool house, flapping his great wings, preening, exposing his orange underparts and white wing patches.

In Spearchucker's kitchen, Mrs. Evelyn Jones, her son, Oliver Wendell Jones, Jr., and the bird-watcher platoon of the moment gasped and babbled in wonderment and confusion.

In the back yard, the star of the show, blown off course in his annual migration from Saskatchewan to Mexico, sensed that the good thing he'd had going for him had come to an end. He filled his belly with all the bird food he could handle and still get airborne, waved his wings in a goodbye salute, and took off for a winter in Acapulco. At four o'clock in the afternoon, Dr. Hawkeye Pierce was watching the '49ers, who were losing to the Lions. To his wife, Mary, he said, "This Willard is a good bread-

and-butter runner, but Frisco hasn't had anybody could really move the ball since Spearchucker retired."

The doorbell rang. "Who the hell is that?" growled Hawkeye. "Whoever it is, I'm not at home. I wanta watch the game. I'll run upstairs and watch from under the bed while you ditch the company."

"Oh, you're so nice," said Mary, "but I'll take care of it."

Moments later Mary, with the guest, entered the bedroom. "Come out from under the bed," she ordered. "It's only Spearchucker."

"Congratulations," said Spearchucker, sounding less than happy. "You got a house guest for a week. I can't go to a motel, the way I look."

Hawkeye, emerging from beneath the bed, inspected his guest and said, "Did you get the number of the truck that ran over you? Christ Almighty, with an eye that black, the rest of you looks white."

"Just get me a drink," ordered Spearchucker.

"What happened?" asked Hawkeye a few minutes later, handing his guest a big bourbon and coke.

"Evelyn was pretty upset about Halfaman busting up the bird-watchers. She's thrown me out for a week."

"Yeah, but how about the truck?"

"It wasn't a truck. Olly, my kid, was bothered about the bird, too, but it might have been okay if I'd kept my mouth shut about the Afro hair. I guess I'll never learn. I thought I could still handle him."

"Grin," suggested Hawkeye.

The phone rang and Oliver Wendell Holmes, Jr., said, "Hey, Uncle Hawk, this is Olly. Is Uncle Tom there?"

"Yeah."

29

"Is he mad?"

"Upset, I guess, but not mad. What's going on with you two?"

"We're having an identity crisis, Uncle Hawk," explained Olly.

"Come on, Olly, for chrissake," said Hawkeye. "Don't give *me* that hosshit. What do you want?"

"Well," said Olly, "I thought I was doing okay but Mama just explained that Daddy could beat me up if he wanted to."

"Yes, Olly," said Hawkeye, "he could. You wanta talk to him?"

"No, not now. Just tell him to come home. Mama's got the clippers out. She's on kind of a kick. She's gonna cut my hair and she's asked Halfaman to dinner and she says my father better get back here, or he'll really be in trouble."

"I'll give him the message," said Uncle Hawkeye.

3
THE RETURN OF
BOOM-BOOM BENNER

IN 1971, twelve years after Doctors Trapper John McIntyre, Hawkeye Pierce, Spearchucker Jones and Duke Forrest started the Finestkind Clinic and Fish Market, Dr. McIntyre, Chief of Cardiovascular Surgery at Spruce Harbor General Hospital, decided that he needed a full-time assistant. His decision came on April 5 after he had performed a particularly long and tedious open heart operation. His assistant, Dr. Hawkeye Pierce, said as they left the operating room, "For chrissake, in the time I spend on one of these cases I could jerk six gallbladders, play nine holes of golf and delight my wife. Why don't you get some young guy to help you?"

"Guess I will," said Trapper. "Maybe I can get that big kid who's working for John Morley at London Hospital. I hear he's a rampaging genius and a touch strange and he wants to come back to the States. John asked me to keep him in mind when I was over there last month."

"What's the guy's name?" asked Hawkeye.

"Walter Benner," said Trapper. "Come to think of it, Morley told me he's from Maine."

"You don't say," replied Hawkeye, who jumped into the shower so Trapper wouldn't see him laughing.

31

That evening Hawkeye sent a brief note to Dr. Walter
Benner at London Hospital:

Dear Boom-Boom:
   Trapper John wants to hire you. Take the job. You and your
wife can stay with me and Mary until you find a place to live.
                                               So long,
                                               Hawk

   Dr. Pierce soon received from London a postcard with
a picture of Big Ben. The card said "boom-boom" and
was signed "Boom-Boom."
   In May, Jerry Cousens, Spruce Harbor General's enterprising PR man, announced the imminent arrival of
a new cardiac surgeon. The press release stated that Dr.
Walter Benner was a native of Port Waldo and a former
Rhodes scholar. He had trained at the Massachusetts
General Hospital and the London Hospital and was, at
the age of thirty-one, a pioneer in the development of
the mechanical heart and an expert in its clinical use.
There was also a paragraph devoted to Dr. Benner's year
as a wide receiver for the Patriots and his prowess at
rugby while at Oxford.
   Dr. Walter Benner, with long black hair waving over
six and a half feet and two hundred and twenty pounds,
arrived with his wife, Vivian, at Logan Airport on a Pan
Am 747 in early June. For the flight to Spruce Harbor the
Benners transferred to a Dehaviland Otter belonging to
the Spruce Harbor and Interisland Air Service. The
plane this day was flown by the airline's owner, the
famed Italian kamikaze pilot, Mr. Wrong Way
Napolitano. Wrong Way seldom pays attention to the
32

passenger list, having no head for business, but he never fails to peruse the cabin in search of good-looking broads. Before takeoff his discerning eye settled on Vivian Benner, and he was about to make a move of some kind when her husband jumped up, extended his hand and said, "Hey, Wrong Way—boom-boom."

"Boom-Boom," said Mr. Napolitano, who twelve years earlier had taught Boom-Boom to fly and learned a language known to an exclusive group, mostly friends of Hawkeye Pierce, as Boom-Boomese. Therefore he added his greeting, "Boom-boom," which, loosely translated, meant "I'm surprised but extremely happy to see you."

Dr. Benner replied, "Boom-Boom," which meant "I'm very glad to see you, too, Wrong Way." Then he nodded toward his wife and said, "Boom-boom."

Wrong Way Napolitano assessed the slim, five foot ten, properly protuberant, gorgeous redhead, extended his hand and exclaimed, "Some jeezly boom-boom," a statement that could be easily translated.

"Oh my God," moaned Vivian Benner. "Everyone assured me there couldn't be any more like Walter."

"Walter who?" asked the pilot.

"Benner, of course."

"Never heard of him," said Wrong Way.

An hour after Wrong Way took off from Logan he brought the Otter in over Thief Island and put down softly at Spruce Harbor International Airport. Dr. and Mrs. Hawkeye Pierce and Dr. Trapper John McIntyre were there to welcome the new heart surgeon.

"Boom-boom, Boom-Boom," said Hawkeye Pierce.

"Boom-Boom," agreed Dr. Benner, who turned to his

33

wife and said, "Viv, this is Hawkeye."

"Boomlay, boomlay, boomlay, BOOM. Finest kind," stated Dr. Pierce.

"I find your quotation from Vachel Lindsay's poem 'The Congo' piquant and poignant, although perhaps a trifle forward, considering your short acquaintance with my wife," said Dr. Benner. "However, I am in total agreement with your evaluation."

"Welcome home, Boom-Boom," said Mrs. Mary Pierce.

Walter Benner, some fifteen inches taller than Mary, lifted her off her feet, kissed her and said, "Boom-boom, Mom."

Trapper John, taking all this in, was having second thoughts about his new colleague. Hawkeye had not briefed Dr. McIntyre.

"Hello, Dr. Benner," said Trapper bravely. "Glad to have you with us."

"Some christly boom-boom, old fellow," said Boom-Boom, suggesting that his basic Maine idiom had been tarnished by years spent in Oxford and London.

"I got all the trouble I need," said Trapper. "I got a wife who milks goats. What kind of a nut are you?"

"Boom-boom," said Boom-Boom.

"Yeah, Boom-boom," said Trapper, who walked to his car shaking his head and muttering under his breath.

Several days later when Dr. Goofus MacDuff, the Medical Director of Spruce Harbor General Hospital, invited Dr. Benner to his office, he was particularly unprepared. Goofus is not well prepared for anything, which is why he is the Medical Director.

"Glad to have you aboard, Doctor," said Goofus, who looks like a toothbrush with hair.

34

"Boom-boom," said Dr. Benner.

"What?" asked Goofus.

"Boom-boom," was the pleasant, smiling response.

"I see in your application that you were born in Port Waldo. I didn't realize that you were from around here."

There was no reply from Dr. Benner, who leaned back in his chair and put his size 13 British footwear on Dr. MacDuff's desk.

"I expect you'll find Spruce Harbor rather quiet after London," offered Goofus, floundering and seeing nothing but enormous shoes.

"Boom-boom," said his visitor.

Confused, Goofus blurted out what is dearest to his heart. "We have staff meeting every Thursday night. Attendance at 50 percent of these meetings is mandatory."

"Omnis Gallia in tres partes divisa est," replied Dr. Benner, who looked absentmindedly out the window at the Finestkind Clinic and Fish Market on the nearby shore.

"What?" inquired Dr. MacDuff.

"The rain in Spain causes wind," Dr. Benner explained. Then, finding the Medical Director speechless, he smiled, said, "Boom-boom" and left.

Dr. Benner, before arriving in Spruce Harbor, had worked in university hospitals at a high research and clinical level. He had not experienced the nuisances and frustrations that plague even the most specialized private practitioners of surgery, particularly in a town like Spruce Harbor. A week after his initial interview with the Medical Director, Boom-Boom received a schedule for Emergency Room coverage and discovered that, once a week, he was on surgical call.

In London Dr. Benner had been the boy wonder. He had addressed international meetings of cardiac surgeons and impressed them with concise accounts of his research and its clinical applications. In his league he was world famous, but in Spruce Harbor he was on call to sew up cuts, most of which didn't need to be sewed up.

Dr. Benner gave long and serious thought, perhaps thirty seconds, to this problem and decided that he should discuss it with the Medical Director. He charged into Dr. MacDuff's office waving the Emergency Room schedule in front of Goofus and said, "Boom-boom."

"What?" asked Goofus, in his usual state of noncomprehension. Clearly Dr. Benner had said, "You may take this piece of paper and place it appropriately."

"Boom-boom," Dr. Benner said again, clearly, slowly, succinctly, malevolently. For emphasis he added, "Boom, bloody boom-boom, you absurd creature."

"You can't talk to me that way," protested Goofus, rather tentatively, since even Goofus had begun to realize that Dr. Benner had already done it.

Dr. MacDuff's office door was open, and by now a small but interested group of secretaries and executive nursing personnel had been attracted to the discussion. One of Dr. Benner's gifts, along with genius and physical strength commensurate with his size, was a fine, rich baritone voice, honed in countless college, university and hospital musical productions. Grasping Goofus by the shirt front with his left hand and holding him six inches off the floor, Boom-Boom gently caressed his victim's face with the Emergency Room roster and sang to him, "I have sounded forth the triumpet that shall never call retreat."

The boom of Boom-Boom's baritone reverberated

through the corridors of the Spruce Harbor General Hospital, and by the time the serenade was over at least twenty people had gathered to watch Dr. Benner release his grasp on Goofus, who fell to the floor in a loose, frightened, indignant heap. Smiling happily, Dr. Benner walked casually out of the Medical Director's office, waved his hand at the multitude and proclaimed, "Boom-boom, everyone. Yes, indeed."

Hawkeye Pierce, informed of the action, arrived just in time to catch Boom-Boom's exit. "Whatcha do?" asked Hawk. "You coldcock him?"

"Hell, no. I just sang to him."

"Look, Boom-Boom, I knew there'd be a ruckus when I saw your name on that ER roster, but maybe you oughta soften the blow for these grunts. They have office-hours mentalities, and they don't dig that we didn't bring you here to help do the scut work. When you gotta problem, for chrissake, just tell me and Trapper and we'll solve it."

"I can't go through life letting you solve all my problems, can I?"

"Look, Boom-Boom, that's not the point. It's just that this is a bush league compared to where you've been, and I know the route better than you do."

"Yeah, Hawk, I know, but I'm just plain offended by a creature like MacDuff. He's outside of my experience. You know I want to live and work here, but if I have to cope with people like him, I'll leave. At the risk of how I sound, you know I can write my own ticket in cardiac surgery."

"I know you can, Boom-Boom, but if you are going to give us a try, you're going to have to understand how things work here. The fact is they work pretty damn

37

well. Nowadays every hospital like this, for lots of reasons, needs a Medical Director. If you can get a real pro for the job, that's ideal, but they're hard to find. Lacking a pro, the best bet is to go with a moron who's happy to shovel what the job calls for. Goofus fills the bill, and Trapper, Duke, Spearchucker and I have manipulated him for years. We wouldn't want to lose him. And then there's the Board of Directors. What you don't know is that in most small hospitals they have more control over clinical progress, or lack of it, than the doctors. So, who are they?"

"I don't know and don't care," said Boom-Boom, "but I suppose I should."

"Traditionally," continued Hawkeye, "in towns like Spruce Harbor they are a bunch of well-meaning Rotarians, businessmen who can think only in dollars and cents and who don't understand the needs of a modern hospital. We've done what doctors all over the country should do. We got Wooden Leg Wilcox in as permanent Chairman of the Board of Directors. He loads the Board with the right people, so we and Wooden Leg run the joint. Leg has the basic business smarts that we lack, and we know the area's medical needs. Between us, we get what we want. You, of course, are a luxury, but you will contribute a lot, and your very presence here will allow us, one way or another, to raise more money to keep things going. Part of the game is to make the people on the Board of Directors think that they are really participating. This is easy. We throw something like "epicardial pacemaker" at the dumb bastards. They can't read it, much less spell it, so they figure it must be great and vote for it. That's how you got here."

"Okay," said Boom-Boom. "I'll try to be loose."

Even though he tried to be loose, Boom-Boom had already generated turmoil. For twelve years the Good People of Spruce Harbor's aristocracy and upper middle class, denied the opportunity to serve (i.e., control) the hospital, and feeling it their due, had been restive. The growth and success of the Spruce Harbor General and the Finestkind Clinic and Fish Market, rather than pleasing them, had in fact frustrated them. Happy and secure in successful mediocrity, an attempt at excellence for its own sake bothered them. Although they couldn't define it, they had the vague realization that if this sort of thing caught on in nonmedical areas, the status quo could get seasick.

The Good People had endured twelve years of intimidation by four surgeons and a one-legged fish dealer. They discussed this endlessly, commiserated about it and achieved total agreement that Doctors Pierce, McIntyre, Forrest and Jones and Mr. Wooden Leg Wilcox were an evil influence. This conclusion was reinforced by the fact that the Spruce Harbor General Hospital, in a national survey, had been selected as one of the two best hospitals anywhere in cities with population of less than 50,000. This was evil because there wasn't a prominent civic leader, industrialist, sky pilot, educator or even an outstanding Jaycee like Billy Sol Estes who could claim one little touch of credit.

So, when Boom-Boom Benner arrived and carried on strangely, the Good People raised their antennae. The Good People had no conception of what Boom-Boom Benner was bringing to Spruce Harbor, nor was there any way that the Good People could have it explained to them. His product was beyond their comprehension and, therefore, suspect. The fact that he'd been a Rhodes scholar and that he had trained at the Massachusetts General and London Hospital cut no ice with the Good People because "Rhodes scholar," "Mass. General" and "London Hospital" had no meaning to the Good People. To the Good People, Boom-Boom was just a new doctor who behaved peculiarly. After all, other doctors came to town and they'd been trained here and there, and what was the difference?

The Good People heard various stories of Boom-Boom, such as his statement to the Congregational minister that the River Jordan is deep and wide but there's lots of broads on the other side. And then there was the incident with the prestigious president of Depositors Trust, George Harrington. George is on the Board of Directors of everything in Maine except the Spruce Harbor General. At a cocktail party Boom-Boom said, "George, I hear you like the broads. Is that true?"

"What?" asked the leading citizen.

"Yeah. Guy told me last week."

"What on earth are you talking about?"

"Guy told me you like young ones. I just wondered. I'm the same way myself. Nice talking to you, old fellow."

Episodes such as these crystallized the determination of the Good People, who went so far as to discuss the possibility of holding meetings to discuss holding meetings to discuss the possibility of rescuing Spruce Harbor General from the infidels. Told of this by one of his many undercover agents, Dr. Hawkeye Pierce said, "Yeah, I know. Don't sweat it. They'll spend a year having meetings trying to decide whether to have meetings. By that time it'll be obvious, even to them, that they'll have to quit or make it a weekly reading of *The Watchtower*."

40

"Huh?" said the undercover agent.

"I figure it could go either way," said Hawkeye.

"Huh?" offered the informant, as Dr. Pierce excused himself.

A month after his arrival in Spruce Harbor, Boom-Boom Benner frustrated the Good People and inactivated them, it is hoped, forever. He put an artificial heart in Halfaman Timberlake. Halfaman, after his third myocardial infarction in as many years, would have died if Dr. Benner had not been in Spruce Harbor with knowledge, training and equipment available before only in a few large medical centers.

The rapid recovery of Mr. Timberlake, a member of the hospital's Board of Directors, was particularly pleasing to the Chairman of the Board, Wooden Leg Wilcox, who said, "Jesus Christ, no way I could ever replace him." When dressed properly, Halfaman looks like a former All-American halfback who has become president of a large bank in Boston or New York. This, combined with the ability to nod his head whenever Mr. Wilcox said, "Ain't that so, Mr. Timberlake?" make him a key member of the Board.

"Another great thing about Halfaman bein' on the Board," explained Wooden Leg one night at the Bay View Cafe, "is any time a meeting runs over an hour, the dumb bastard starts jumping around like he's got groin pheasants and that's all the excuse I need to adjourn the meetin'."

On a Saturday eighteen days after the historic operation, while newsmen from everywhere waited to interview him, Halfaman was spirited out of the hospital by Wooden Leg Wilcox, who drove him directly to Spruce Harbor's only whorehouse. There Bette Bang Bang, Mat-

41

tress Mary and Made Marion welcomed their all-time champion customer with, describing the welcome with restraint, open arms. Mr. Wilcox then joined Boom-Boom, Hawkeye and Trapper John at the Bay View Cafe, where the surgeons were nervously nursing martinis and looking at their watches. An hour later the call came from Bette Bang Bang, who told Wooden Leg, "He's better'n ever. He took care of all three of us, and he ain't even breathin' ha'hd."

"Congratulations, Boom-Boom," said Hawkeye. "You did it. It will once again be possible for a hard-working whore to make a living in Spruce Harbor."

"Boom-boom," said Dr. Benner, obviously pleased, and excused himself to return to the hospital. Then Wooden Leg had a crisis at the fish market, so Hawkeye and Trapper John were left alone at the bar.

"Okay," said Trapper. "Tell me the story of Boom-Boom Benner."

A faraway look appeared in Hawkeye's eye, which, like the rest of him, was now middle-aged. "Okay," he agreed, "but only because it's raining and I can't play golf. Buy me another drink."

Trapper ordered the drink and said, "Talk."

"Boom-Boom," said Dr. Pierce, "is one of eight children belonging, somewhat, to Bertie and Jennie Benner over in Port Waldo, and he's the only one who can get through doors and around corners. If Bertie Benner could shoot his IQ, Palmer and Nicklaus would be driving trucks. Boom-Boom's mother, Jennie, is a lot smarter than Bertie, but she grew up in total poverty, had no education and never became adept at anything except sexual intercourse—and I hear she was pretty good. I don't know for sure where Boom-Boom came from—

maybe he was a long-shot chromosomal collision between Bertie and Jennie, but I doubt it. The Benners
were always "on the State," as the saying goes. I know
a social worker who used to have them as a case, and I've
always figured that, in his zeal, he provided us with our
new heart surgeon, but it's just a hunch."

"Anyway, by the time Boom-Boom was ten years old
he'd become a problem. In a more enlightened area the
school system would have adjusted to him, but in Port
Waldo, no way. Christ, at ten he knew more than any of
the grade school teachers, but they wouldn't let him
start high school till he was thirteen. By then he knew
more than any high school teacher. I think they clocked
him around 170–180 on the IQ machine. There wasn't
anybody for him to talk to at home, or anywhere else, but
he took to hanging around Jimmy Richards' drugstore,
and he learned more about pharmacy than Jimmy, so
Jimmy let him run the store. When he was about fourteen he decided that talking to anybody in Port Waldo
was a waste of time, so he started saying 'boom-boom' in
response to everybody and everything. Along with the
boom-boom he'd throw in ridiculous, meaningless
rhymes. Believe me, he had the citizens some shook up,
and when he tried to burn down the high school, that
tore it."

"Why in hell," asked Trapper, "did he try to burn
down the high school?"

"Looking back, I figure he wanted attention—any
kind of attention. He wanted to change the game. Sure,
he was a genius, but he was also a kid, and he must have
decided that any change would be an improvement. He
got caught. For chrissake, if he'd really wanted to burn
down the high school, he could have done it."

"What happened then?" asked Trapper.

Hawkeye had to interrupt his story because, for thirty seconds, he was overcome with laughter. When able to continue, he said, "Well, I got this secondhand from Jimmy Richards. Nobody knew what the hell to do with him. The grunts wanted to put him in the license plate academy. At this point Doggy Moore stepped in. The reason Doggy Moore is still a more valuable doctor than you, me or Boom-Boom is that nothing escapes him and he never lets anything bad happen. So Doggy rigged it for Boom-Boom to go to the fool farm in Augusta instead of State Prison."

Hawkeye started to laugh again.

"What's funny?" asked Trapper.

"They had this hearing at the Court House in Spruce Harbor. The judge, Jim Carr, our golfing friend whom we call the hanging judge, told Boom-Boom that he'd been spared the license plate academy and would go to the fool farm. Jim asked if Boom-Boom had anything to say. Boom-Boom stood up. 'Yes, sir, I do,' he replied. 'Say it,' said the judge. Boom-Boom's statement was, 'Tear my tattered ensign down. Long has it waved on high.'

"The judge turned to a bailiff and said, 'Get that stupid sonovabitch the hell out of here.' I reminded him of that on the 16th the other day, and he blew a two-foot putt."

"So how did Boom-Boom make out at the fool farm?" Trapper asked, and ordered another drink.

"Oh, like a tall dog. Most of the professional personnel up there speak English with a Balkan brogue, and "boom-boom" lost something when translated into their native tongues. The only conclusion they reached was that he had a limited vocabulary. And, of course, they were confused by his religious fervor. The institution's theological program rivals, or may exceed, its psychiatric effort. Boom-Boom went to all religious services and disrupted them by getting up at five-minute intervals and chanting in a booming monotone, 'I can beat any son of a whore in the house at dominoes vobiscum.' Then he'd sit down and look very devout."

"So how'd he get out?" asked Trapper.

"Doggy Moore got him out, and I remember the day after he got out. It was a Saturday in early April the first year I was in practice. I was playing cribbage with Jimmy Richards in the back room of his drugstore. It was snowing to beat hell and I was bitching about the weather because I prefer golf to cribbage.

" 'Spring is practically here,' Jimmy Richards said. 'Guaranteed. Sarah Williams was in and told me Halfaman Timberlake was sitting on her back fence this morning, performing the rites of spring. You know as well as I do, when Halfaman goes public, spring is upon us.' "

" 'Yeah,' I said. 'I'm aware of the legend, but I'm not convinced.'

"Jimmy got up, went out front and came back with a sign from his window. 'Maybe this'll make you believe the sap is rising,' he said.

"The sign announced the formation of a Kum Duble Club at the Methodist Church. 'Wonder what they'll do at their first meeting?' I asked, not really caring.

" 'I should imagine,' said Jimmy, 'they'll hold time trials and establish handicaps.'

" 'I shouldn't wonder,' I muttered, and at this moment Doggy Moore burst in, obviously upset, just swearing and not defining his unhappiness. When he defined it, even I agreed that the sap was rising. Doggy'd gotten Boom-Boom out of the peculiar parlor the day before, and the first thing he'd done was try to rape Anastasia Higgins."

"Who's Anastasia Higgins?" asked Trapper.

"A boon to all mankind," Hawkeye assured Trapper, "which I pointed out to Doggy. 'I know,' moaned Doggy, 'but Boom-Boom had a great need and he didn't think to ask, so Anastasia thought he was going for her pocketbook. By the time she'd figured it out, she'd made her move and had to stay with it. I got her talked out of making trouble only because, without me, she'd have twenty kids and permanent clap. But, what the hell am I going to do with Boom-Boom?'

" 'Well, Doggy,' I said, 'I got no use for nuts and neurotics but I keep an open mind on screwballs. You got no choice. You gotta take him into your home.' "

"I knew Doggy'd taken bigger gambles into his home, so I waited and watched his reaction very carefully.

" 'Make you a deal, Hawkeye,' said Doggy. 'Me and Emma will take him during the week if you and Mary will take him weekends.' "

"And that's why he calls Mary 'Mom,' " said Trapper.

"Yeah. Jesus, when I told Mary she went through the roof. 'Five kids,' she yelled, 'and we're going to have Boom-Boom Benner on weekends. You are out of your mind, and I won't stand for it.'

" 'Boom-Boom will be down Friday night,' I told her. 'I'm sorry, honey, but there isn't a damn thing I can do about it.'

"On the way home that Friday night I picked up the genius and said, 'Boom-Boom, my wife doesn't want you around. We may both get shot when we go through the door.'

" 'Boom-boom,' he said. I had been hoping for more.

46

" 'You've reached a crossroads in your interesting career,' I told him. 'You are a genius. The question remains whether you are crazy. If you aren't crazy, Doggy and I will arrange an outlet for your big brain. I'll invest one weekend in finding out about you. I got no use for nuts.'

" 'Boom-boom,' he said, and I was figuring him for a real nut, but we drove into the yard, and Billy, who was eight or nine then, ran out and said, 'Hi ya, Boom-Boom. Will you play baseball with me?'

" 'Sure, Billy,' Boom-Boom said."

At this point Dr. Pierce sipped his drink and looked away because, as Trapper John detected, there were tears in his eyes.

"Pardon the emotion," said Hawkeye, "but I can't help it. From that moment on, Mary and I became his parents. We're only what—fifteen or sixteen years older than he—but he'd never really had parents or a home. It was easy. The scholarships came. There was no real expense, and I'm some goddamn proud of him. Sure, I admit he's peculiar in spots, but you don't have any doubt about his ability, or what he can do for us, do you?"

"Hell, no," said Trapper. "As far as I'm concerned, he's number one anywhere and having him here is fantastic good luck. I just wanted the background. How come you never told me about him before he came?"

"I was saving it," said Hawkeye with a grin.

Boom-Boom Benner, proving that he wasn't just lucky, plugged in two more artificial hearts in the week following Halfaman's discharge and rehabilitation. In the midst of his total involvement in the preoperative, operative and postoperative care of these patients, he was bothered by demands that he see patients in the Emergency Room. When the cardiac action died down,

47

Dr. Benner said to Dr. Pierce, "Look, Hawkeye, I want that moron, MacDuff, off my back. I have no intention of covering the Emergency Room, and if that doesn't please you, just tell me, and I'll be on my way."

"Boom-Boom," said Hawk, "keep trying to understand the league. As I've told you, our inner group and Wooden Leg run this joint, but we are dealing with a bunch of lamebrains. They can be managed or faked out, one way or another, but, because they are lamebrains, it's a mistake ever to run at them head-on. When you fake them out, they are sullen because they figure they've been faked out. They don't understand the technique, but they hold still. But hit them head-on and they know what to do. Goofus and half the staff would rather make you cover the Emergency Room than save five extra lives a day. That's how their minds work. Once you understand this and adjust to it, it's not a problem."

"It's still a problem to me," said Boom-Boom. "I hear you talking, but you haven't told me what to do!"

"Obviously," said Hawkeye, "what to do is scare everyone in the Emergency Room witless so they'll leave you alone. Don't resign. Get fired. It's so simple. I don't see why I have to explain it to a genius."

"Boom-boom," said Dr. Benner, and Hawkeye thought he detected challenge and anticipation in his protégé's demeanor.

Dr. Benner, while at London Hospital, had been farmed to Peking for a month, where he had allowed his genius to shine upon the Chinese. While in Peking he had become interested, in an amused way, in the technique of acupuncture. This is a very valuable and useful technique based upon an age-old medical dictum which is: Stick needles in a guy every time he complains about something and pretty soon the guy's going to stop complaining.

After his talk with Hawkeye, Boom-Boom went to see Wooden Leg Wilcox, discussed his Emergency Room problem, and suggested that the Emergency Room might provide an opportunity to gain further experience in acupuncture. Mr. Wilcox, who had left his original right leg on Okinawa in 1945 and who was active in the Maine Amputees Association, expressed enthusiastic interest in acupuncture and gave Boom-Boom an ice pick.

A week later, when Dr. Benner was on call, Mr. Wilcox, Chairman of the Board of Directors, brought to the Emergency Room a weekend guest who was having severe abdominal pain, dizzy spells and a splitting headache.

Boom-Boom Benner greeted Mr. Wilcox and the patient, took the history and then asked the nurse to remove the patient's right shoe. Pulling an ice pick from his inside coat pocket, Boom-Boom enthusiastically stabbed the patient's right foot. The patient screamed.

Wooden Leg Wilcox, within the limits of his ability to do it, jumped up and down indignantly and yelled, "What the——. Why you crazy——."

Turning to a nurse, he ordered, "Get Goofus. Get him down here."

Summoned by the Chairman of the Board, Goofus appeared immediately. "Why you got this crazy bastard working in here?" demanded the Chairman.

"Well, gee," said Goofus, "everybody's supposed——"

"Look, you jerk," interrupted Wooden Leg, "if I ever hear this crazy bastard is workin' in heah, you're gonna be used up."

"Well, okay. Sure, Leg," said Goofus.

"Hey, Doc," said the patient to Boom-Boom. "I feel better already. How about hittin' me one more time?"

Boom-Boom, with all his strength, drove the ice pick into the lower part of the patient's artificial limb.

"How's that?" he asked.

"Oh, Doc," sighed the patient, "finest kind. I think I'm gonna live."

4

DRAGONS

ONE never knows what'll happen on Monday mornings at Spruce Harbor Medical Center. I was in the coffee shop, seated with Goofus MacDuff, my Medical Director, and Dr. Ferenc Ovari. At a nearby table were Duke Forrest, Spearchucker Jones, Boom-Boom Benner, Trapper John McIntyre and Hawkeye Pierce.

There was a lull in their conversation. I sensed that something was about to happen and just hoped it wouldn't be too bad. Spearchucker Jones arose, walked purposefully toward our table and, addressing Goofus MacDuff, said, "Hey, Health King, you wanna fight?"

For some time now Goofus has been on many committees planning the largesse of health which the government is laying upon us. He has even learned to say "at this point in time," "ongoing" and "study in depth." This is the basic lexicon of health planners. Goofus uses these magic expressions so often that Health King is truly an apt name.

"Why should I want to fight?" asked Goofus in a quavering voice, sort of scrunching over to hide behind the bulk of Rex Eatapuss.

"Because I heard what you said."

"What did I say?"

"You said 'hopefully,' 'study in depth' and 'at this point

51

in time' all in one sentence. We can't have that kind of talk. You hear me, boy?"

"Y-yes, sir."

"Okay, I'll overlook it this time, but be damn careful, Health King."

Spearchucker had no more than returned to his table when Hawkeye Pierce got up, came over, sat down in Dr. Ovari's ample lap and told the surprised psychologist, "Rex Eatapuss, I love you."

"What I been tellin' you?" I heard Spearchucker say. "That honky's softer than a sneakerful of grits."

Rex Eatapuss sort of squealed. "Listen to him squeal," Hawkeye exhorted his following. "He loves me, too." Hawk pinched Rex's plump cheek and got up, saying, "I'll see you later, sweetie."

"You are a psychopath. You are a deviate," proclaimed Rex Eatapuss.

After a few moments of silence while no one seemed to have much to say, the conversation at the surgeons' table turned to Duke Forrest's weekend. Actually he and his wife had spent two days at the Park Entrance Motel in Bar Harbor and played golf at Kebo Valley. Duke chose, however, to tell a different story, which was:

On the previous Wednesday he and Mrs. Penelope Flewelling, a witch friend of Hawkeye's, had flown to Ulan Bator, Outer Mongolia. The flight time on Penelope's new broomstick had been just under twenty minutes. Reason for trip: As club champion of Wawenock Harbor Country Club, Duke had been invited to play in the Outer Mongolian Open, which he won with a score of 72. Seventy-two consecutive holes in one.

"A record that should hold up," said Boom-Boom Benner.

Rex Eatapuss and Goofus (Health King) MacDuff left the coffee shop after hearing of this feat. They seemed disturbed by this and other events of the morning.

That very afternoon two men appeared in the surgical waiting room of the Finest Kind Clinic and demanded to see Doctors Pierce and Forrest immediately. A secretary politely asked them to wait, but they avowed that they would not wait because they were authorized to take Dr. Pierce and Dr. Forrest to the State Hospital in Augusta where they had been committed for psychiatric examination.

The secretary just laughed, but as the two sheriff's deputies advanced upon the doctors' inner office, she stopped laughing and ran to get Hawkeye and Spearchucker. When help arrived the deputies were standing in front of Duke's desk, and Duke was explaining that he was a dangerous maniac and their best bet was to cut out quickly before he took punitive action.

"What's the problem, George?" Hawk asked one of the deputies, with whom he'd grown up.

"We gotta take you and him, Hawk. Dr. MacDuff and Dr. Ovari signed papers on you."

"You better get out of here, George, because if you don't you're likely to get hurt. Does that give you any kind of message?"

"Unless," added Spearchucker, "you have butterfly nets. Naturally, if you got butterfly nets we wouldn't dream of interfering."

The deputies were silent. "Maybe we could save time and examine them for butterfly nets," suggested Hawkeye.

"Indeed, we could do that," said Spearchucker, who seemed attracted by the idea.

The idea didn't seem to attract the deputies. "You ain't heard the last of this, Hawkeye," said George.

"Now," said Spearchucker to Duke, "will you please explain what this is all about?"

"I haven't the faintest idea. If Goofus and Rex Eatapuss think I'm crazy, y'all ask them. I got patients waiting."

Later that afternoon Hawkeye barged into the office of Dr. Goofus MacDuff and said, "Goofus, sit and talk to me. We need to discuss this and that."

"Gee," said Goofus, "that sounds like a good idea."

"You better believe it is. What's this crap about having Duke and me committed?"

"Well, gee, I don't know why you're upset. We didn't have any choice. Everybody knows about you and you must have heard about Duke Forrest."

"Heard what?"

"Dr. Forrest spent half an hour in the hospital coffee shop this morning telling everybody he'd spent four days in Outer Mongolia—some place called Oven Butter."

"You mean Ulan Bator," Hawk prompted him. "That's the capital of Outer Mongolia."

"Yes, of course. Duke says he won the Ulan Bator Open. Says he shot seventy-two consecutive holes in one."

"Amazing," agreed Hawkeye. "All-time record. But I don't seem to understand why you are so upset. Why not rejoice that a member of our staff has achieved such distinction?"

Unruffled, Goofus patiently explained how Duke claimed that he'd flown to Outer Mongolia in nineteen minutes on a broomstick driven by a witch named Pamela Fleming.

"You seem to have trouble with proper names, Goofus," said Hawkeye. "Not Pamela Fleming. The witch's name is Mrs. Penelope Flewelling. I've known the broad all my life. She lives in a cave beneath a tree with a hollow trunk on the edge of the saltmarsh in Crabapple Cove."

"Gee," said Goofus, "you really are crazy. I've wondered."

"Wondered what, Goofus?"

"If you're crazy."

"Goofus, I just don't understand you," said Hawkeye. "Apparently you've blown the whole deal. The fact is, Penelope took Duke over on her new stick, which has eight forward gears. She's been breaking it in. If she opened that thing up, she figures she could make Ulan Bator in maybe fourteen minutes. I hope we have everything straightened out, Goofus. See you."

Hawkeye drove home, laughing most of the way. As his children grew, he'd gone the good daddy route and read children's books at bedtime. As time passed, he'd had Dr. Seuss, particularly, and most children's literature right up to his ears. He had, therefore, created his own stories, which were completely ridiculous, but telling them stimulated him more than "Ant and Bee." His stories seemed to stimulate his children, too. Duke, he knew, had heard Penelope Flewelling stories from Willy and Steve Pierce. Duke, obviously, in a quixotic moment, had stolen one for use in the coffee shop. The story of seventy-two holes in one at the Ulan Bator Open, a Hawkeye original, was a favorite of Dr. Pierce's golf-oriented children.

"I can't believe it, though," Hawk said to himself. "I can't believe that anyone could take anything so silly seriously. On the other hand, I'm beginning to understand. People around here have little exposure and little imagination. A surgeon, like Duke, is viewed with a sort of awe. Duke thought he was just amusing the folks and it never occurred to him that anyone would not be amused. He overrates the troops, and I guess he's too good an actor. It'd be a pity not to take advantage of this and get a few laughs."

That evening Hawkeye was reading a collection of papers about chronic pancreatitis when the phone rang. Jim Holden, his lawyer, the most sure-footed young mouthpiece in Maine, said, "What the hell are you and Duke up to?"

"You mean what?"

"The Judge called. Goofus and Rex Eatapuss are trying to place you and Duke in the peculiar parlor."

"That should be fun."

"Look, Hawkeye. I know you think it's funny and so does the Judge, but he can't ignore it. He's going out of his way to straighten things out, mostly because you've been grabbing him on the golf course and he can't get even if you're in the fool farm. He wants an informal hearing with you, me, Duke, Goofus and Rex. He says he has to have two psychiatrists from the fool farm present and he says if you and Duke keep up this nonsense he'll stick you both away for fifty years. We're all going to meet the Judge in his office at ten o'clock on Wednesday. Be there and don't screw up, or I'll give you to him."

Judge Jim Carr looked forward to Wednesday because he, unlike grunts like Goofus and Rex Eatapuss, knew the whole thing was a joke. He hoped Hawkeye and Duke wouldn't overdo it, but secretly he hoped they'd provide an interesting morning.

56

In the Judge's chambers Goofus told Judge Carr of Duke's alleged participation in a golf tournament in Ulan Bator, and of the nineteen-minute ride on Mrs. Flewelling's broomstick.

"Dr. Forrest," asked Judge Carr when Goofus was through, "would you care to comment?"

"Judge, you ever played Ulan Bator?" asked Duke.

"No," the judge admitted. "But let's get to the point, Dr. Forrest. You have stated that you shot seventy-two consecutive holes in one. This defies belief. Your sanity, as a result, has been questioned."

"Mrs. Flewelling just kind of kept guiding them balls," explained Duke. "She can make herself invisible, you know. Why, she'd just glide in on that new broom, pick up my drive in midair and deliver it to the cup."

"Dr. Forrest, this is an informal hearing. You are not under oath, but it could come to that. Are you prepared to repeat this story in a court?"

"Of course," agreed Duke.

"Very well," the judge said. "Dr. Pierce, may I ask you a few questions?"

"Shoot, Judge," Hawkeye said.

"Dr. Pierce, have you also played the course at Ulan Bator?"

"Sure. Ever since Penelope got her new broomstick it's a quick shot over there, and Penelope wants to break it in. Nice course. Greens don't hold too well, but I can get home at five, ride over with Penelope, tee off at five-twenty, play nine, fly back, have a drink and eat supper at seven-thirty."

"The course isn't very crowded, I guess," observed Judge Carr.

"Hell, no. Only three members."

"Who's the pro at Ulan Bator?"

"Ghengis Khanstein. Used to be big on the Siberian tour, but he got the yips with his putter, like Hogan."

"They're crazy, Judge," said Goofus MacDuff.

"Hey, Hawkeye," said Duke. "Maybe we're in trouble. You better show the judge your letter from General MacArthur. He put in a nice word for you. Might help out now."

"It might," Hawkeye agreed. "Only fair, after what I done for Doug."

"Gentlemen," said Judge Carr, "enough is enough. Let's leave General MacArthur out of it."

"Judge," interjected Hawk's lawyer, Jim Holden, "I request that a letter from General Douglas MacArthur be presented as a testimonial to the character and sanity of Dr. Benjamin F. Pierce."

"Okay, boys," said the Judge, "let's not get silly. Just what did General MacArthur have to say?"

"How Hawkeye Pierce won World War II single-handed, with the help of Mrs. Penelope Flewelling," stated Attorney Holden. "We'll subpoena General Eisenhower's records, too, if we have to."

"Gee, Judge, I think the lawyer's crazy, too," said Goofus.

"Shut the hell up, Goofus," admonished Judge Carr, who then asked Dr. Pierce, "Is this story of how you won World War II single-handed something you can get through in less than half an hour?"

"If I hurry."

"Proceed quickly."

"Well," Hawkeye said, "most people around here will recall that, up until about thirty years ago, the coast of Maine, particularly Muscongus Bay, was infested with

58

dragons. A lot of people don't realize that if it hadn't been for me and Mrs. Penelope Flewelling the State of Maine would be up to its ass in dragons, even Aroostook County."

"Informal though this hearing may be," said the judge, "watch your language."

"Sure, Jim," Hawk agreed. "Anyway, as a kid I had a dragon boat, that fourteen-foot dory I still got and a five-hoss Johnson, and I took up dragon crunching. One way or another, with Penelope's help, I crunched every jeezely dragon in Muscongus Bay. I got so good I could handle the little ones, the twenty- to thirty-footers, all alone. If they ran over thirty feet, Mrs. Flewelling was around to help out. She had this sharp-pointed broom-stick she used against dragons. By the Jesus, when she hit them dragons going seven hundred, maybe eight hundred miles an hour, you better believe they folded quick. As it turned out, after losing to me and Penelope for three or four years, the survivors took off and went to Europe, which is why I made it possible for our troops to invade France on D-Day."

"Will you explain that, please?" asked the judge.

"Sure. When I got drafted into the Army they asked me what I was good at and I told them dragon crunching so they classified me as a 2750 A, which means Dragon Cruncher, First Class. All I did the first two years in the Army was sit around waiting for dragons to crunch, and I was kinda bored. But then it come to be early June 1944 and they put me and my boat on a big plane and flew me to England where they took me to a house in London, 10 Downing Street I think it was, and introduced me to General Eisenhower and Mr. Winston Churchill, a limey politician who gave me a cigar and a shot of brandy.

" 'Nice to meet you fellers,' I said. 'In what way may I be of service?'

" 'Well,' Ike explained, 'we're landing in France in a few days and it turns out the pretzel benders have hired a thousand dragons to guard the beaches and repel our invasion. Personally, I have no experience with dragons and I'm fearful lest their presence have a deleterious, maybe even fatal effect on our troops.'

" 'Me, too,' said Mr. Churchill.

" 'Well,' I said, 'I shouldn't wonder but what you fellers want me to crunch those dragons, or leastways run them off.'

" 'Private Pierce,' Ike said, 'you pierce right to the heart of a subject, don't you?'

"I had to agree, of course. 'Gimme two days and I'll solve the dragon problem, Ike,' I told him.

" 'Bless you, Private Pierce,' said the general.

" 'Oh, wizard,' said the Prime Minister."

Goofus MacDuff was becoming restive. "Do we have to listen to any more of this?" he asked the Judge.

"I don't know about you, Goofus," said Judge Carr, "but when I have the chance to hear, first-hand, of history in the making, I listen. You may continue, Dr. Pierce."

"Well," Hawkeye continued, "I won't string it out. Mrs. Flewelling was hanging around close so I decided not to bother with my boat. She had a new two-seater for a stick and we left right from 10 Downing Street for the Normandy beaches. It took us two days, me crunching them and her stabbing them with her stick, but we de-dragoned that whole coast. Without our efforts, obviously, the invasion would have been impossible."

"Obviously," agreed Judge Carr. "But how does General MacArthur get into the story?"

"Well, after I got through in Normandy, Ike let me come home on furlough, and said to have a good time so long as he could find me if he needed me. So one day I'm sitting in the Tea House of the March Wind—you know that joint Ace Kimball still runs down on Ocean Street —I was having my third tea when the phone rings and Ace says, 'Hawk, it's for you,' and I answer and a guy asks, 'Is this Private Pierce?'

" 'Ayuh,' I said.

" 'This is General Douglas MacArthur,' the guy says.

" 'How they goin', Doug?' I asked him.

" 'No good,' Doug says. 'We got a dragon problem out here in the Pacific. Ike says you are right handy with dragons.'

" 'They give me little trouble,' I told him. 'What is the nature of your dragon problem?'

" 'It is the Grand Dragon,' explained Doug. 'This dragon runs around three hundred feet in length and breathes fire so hot that it melts aircraft carriers. He can submerge for hours at a time. Shells and bullets bounce off him. He is wiping out our fleet. At night he crawls ashore and eats the planes on our airstrips. He is, in fact, a very tough dragon and he is impeding our war effort.'

" 'Doug,' I said, 'I dunno. This sounds like maybe too much dragon, even for me. Perhaps you could try some-one else.'

" 'Soldier,' said the General, 'a plane will pick you up in Bangor. Bring anything you need, but be on that plane or you know what it's gonna be!'

" 'Yes, sir,' I said and drove home and went through the hollow tree into Mrs. Flewelling's cave where I ex-plained the situation. Well, this was one time Penelope

61

let me down. She outright refused to have anything to do with a three-hundred-foot dragon, so I loaded my dragon boat onto my old man's pickup and he drove me to Bangor and three days later I landed in Manila and met Doug. Doug said the Grand Dragon was cruising a few miles offshore and was probably figuring to have supper at a nearby airstrip and the estimate of his average appetite came to six fighter planes and a couple of bombers.

"So I gassed up that old five-hoss Johnson and headed the dory to sea. Pretty soon I saw a big wave and a lot of foam and something that looked like a submarine except it had six-foot spines all along its back and I knew this had to be the Grand Dragon. He gave me a dirty look and breathed some fire as a sort of warning, but I kept right on going. He just watched me, and finally I pulled up alongside of him.

" 'Hi, Dragon,' I said. 'How they goin'?'

" 'Finestkind,' he replied, and asked, 'What are you? A nut? They don't even dare send a battleship out when I'm around.'

" 'So I hear,' I said. 'I'm Hawkeye Pierce. Perhaps you've heard of me?'

" 'Are you from Maine? Are you the famous dragon cruncher?' he asked.

" 'None other,' I assured him, and asked, 'What's your name?'

" 'Big Sid,' he said with a grin that revealed a tremendous mouthful of teeth the size of telephone poles. And then he asked, 'Hey, Hawk, you gonna give me a try?'

" 'Look, Sid,' I said, 'let us understand one another right here and now. I am a fair country dragon cruncher, but I am out of shape and I have had no experience with dragons of your type build. Let me assure you that this is purely a friendly visit. I have not come to fight. I have come to bargain.'

" 'Go on, I'm listening,' roared Big Sid.

" 'I hear you have a dietary weakness. I hear you like airplanes,' I said to the Grand Dragon.

" 'Your information is correct,' he assured me. 'What's your offer? I'm some hungry.'

" 'Could I interest you in the entire Japanese air force?'

"Big Sid, the Grand Dragon, thought for a moment before answering: 'I've already eaten part of it. Them Zeros is tasty but they don't stay with you. You gotta do better than that.'

" 'Well,' I told him, 'there'll be a lot of surplus outdated planes on our side once the war's over. I'll arrange for you to get them, and all the surplus outdated planes for the next hundred years. How's that grab you?'

" 'First rate,' he said. 'What have I got to do?'

" 'Very little,' I told him. 'All I want you to do is cruise up to Japan and breathe on some city about ten days from now. I'll let you know the exact time and place and we'll work it out so one of our bombers drops a bomb at the same time. You head for Japan, and I'll be in touch with you.'

"A week later a submarine surfaced at night a few miles off the Japanese city of Hiroshima. Two miles farther out, Big Sid, the Grand Dragon, was lolling leisurely in the waves.

"My dory with the five-hoss Johnson was launched from the sub and I went to see Big Sid. 'Here's the deal, Sid,' I explained. 'Tomorrow at seven o'clock I want you to crawl ashore at Hiroshima. Wait until you see a

63

bomber overhead and wait till you see a big bomb drop. Then I want you to take the deepest breath you can and blast off. You got it?' I asked.

"'A piece of cake,' he said and grinned.

"'I sure hope so,' I said. 'If this act swings, you're booked at Nagasaki the week after next. That should do it.'

"Well, as everybody knows, Hiroshima and Nagasaki were wiped off the map. It is not, however, common knowledge that the atom bomb wasn't invented until 1950. At Hiroshima and Nagasaki it was my buddy, Big Sid, the Grand Dragon, just blowing off a little steam and giving our scientists time to perfect the bomb."

At the conclusion of this moving tale, Judge Carr, so overcome with emotion that words failed him, rose from his chair, approached Hawkeye and solemnly shook his hand, as did Lawyer Holden and Duke Forrest. "I'm so very, very proud of you, Hawkeye," the Judge was able to say, finally, in a voice choked with emotion.

"But what about committing him?" demanded Goofus.

"MacDuff, I'm thinking of having *you* put away," said Judge Carr as he left his chambers and departed for the Spruce Harbor Country Club.

"But," squealed Rex Eatapuss, "Pierce is a deviate."

"A what?" asked Judge Carr.

"A deviate," asserted Rex.

"Oh, I know what you mean," said the Judge. "His drives deviate slightly to the left. You really mean he's a hooker, because his left wrist is a little limp."

"But," expostulated Rex, though getting no further.

"Get that hunky outta here, Henry," Judge Carr instructed the bailiff.

5
CHRISTMAS STORY

EDDIE STEMKOWSKY, the notorious Jumping Polack of Lincoln County, now teaches history at Port Waldo High School, where Hawkeye and I matriculated. My surgeons, the former Swampmen, are a tightly knit group. Their inner circle is small. How one gets to be a member is impossible to define. The Jumping Polack, for whatever reason, is in. Possibly because he jumped, naked, into a snowbank from a second-story girls' dormitory window as an undergraduate at the University of Maine at Orono.

Eddie is married to Alice, a helluva nice broad he met when he was going to the University. They have two little kids, a small house, two VW's, two jobs and a pure-bred Dutch-type dog called a Keeshond that produces seven or eight puppies every eight months. The puppies are worth a hundred and fifty bucks each. Obviously they have economic significance.

Eddie's dog, fascinatingly named Arf-Arf, calved eight times in November 1973. One night in early December Eddie and Alice hit a patch of ice and left the road. The Volkswagen protected neither of their right femurs. Truly a family accident. Both immobilized, out of work, out of action for at least three months. Money still coming in, but not enough to cover all expenses. Minor tragedy, negligible in fact, but their friends had to help.

Mrs. Lucinda McIntyre gathered to her growing bosom not only the two Stemkowsky children. She also took in Arf-Arf and the eight puppies, worth twelve hundred dollars if the puppy market was right. Trapper John, visiting Eddie and Alice in the hospital, expressed his approval of Lucinda's act of kindness. "I like dogs and Polacks," he told them.

Lucinda set out to sell the puppies. She advertised them in the *Press Herald* and the *Boston Globe*. There were no takers. She talked to pet shops, which offered only fifty to seventy-five a puppy, explaining that merchandising a puppy is enhanced by allowing the customer to see the puppy. Lots of puppy sales, it seems, are on the spur of the moment. Newspaper ads for puppies, she was told, are particularly ineffective during energy crises. Nobody asked for an explanation of this and none was offered, to the best of my knowledge.

Lucinda had also taken over the Stemkowsky family finances. As Christmas approached she realized that there wasn't quite enough money to pay all the bills and buy presents for the children. She decided on December 24 to start her own pet shop in the window of Stiff Standing Hooper's real estate office, which is right next to his outstanding funeral parlor on Main Street in Spruce Harbor. Lucinda, along with other activities, is a part-time real estate saleslady. She had all eight puppies in a big basket where the last-minute Christmas shoppers could see them. The sign said: "Keeshonds for sale."

Let me make it quite clear that I never heard of a Keeshond until Eddie and Alice came up with Arf-Arf. I'm told they are very large in Holland. What I do know is that a seven-week-old Keeshond puppy is about the

66

most lovable, cuddly little ball of silver gray face-licking fur you'll find anywhere. Certainly the best of anything that ever appeared in the window of Stiff Standing Hooper's real estate office.

Lucinda opened her pet shop at 10 A.M. She told me about the first sale and the whole crazy business at a New Year's Eve party. "Oh, Hook," she said, "I'd no more than put them in the window than a young service man, Air Force I think, and his wife and two little boys stopped. They were an awfully nice looking young couple. I think the boy played basketball for us a few years ago, real nice looking kids, maybe seven or eight. I began to get this awful feeling, watching those kids look at the puppies. I watched the parents. I just knew what they were saying with their eyes and they said something to each other, all the time looking at the kids and the puppies. And they tried to get the kids moving but they just kept staring fascinated at the puppies. Finally the father talked to the older boy. I just know Mommy and Daddy were on a tight budget. They were embarrassed to come in and ask how much. They decided maybe they could afford twenty, maybe thirty dollars. Daddy told the boy to come in and ask how much.

"I'd already made up my mind those kids were going to have a puppy and I was going to say twenty bucks, the hell with it, but just before the kid came I saw Spear-chucker Jones come out of the bank across the street. He, too, was attracted by the puppies and, as the kid came in, I realized he'd been monitoring the scene, just as I had. The older boy came in and his little brother followed him. They looked into the basket and, well, you know kids and puppies, they were just dying to pick one of them up, but they didn't and finally the older boy asked, 'How much for a puppy?' The look on his face, wish you could have seen it, and, well, you know me, but I had a hunch, so I said, 'A hundred and fifty dollars.'

"I almost broke down. The smaller boy had tears in his eyes. Corny, isn't it? Yeah, well, so it is, but it happened. In a choked-up little voice the kid said, 'Thank you,' and he and his brother walked out. I watched him tell his parents and saw their look of frustration—more than that, despair. And then I saw my main man make his move and I knew, I just knew my hunch had paid off. Spearchucker Jones walked up to the couple, and I opened the door so I could hear. 'I'm Dr. Jones,' he said. 'Didn't I see you play basketball a few years ago?' he asked the airman, and the young man said, 'Yes,' obviously proud to be recognized by Dr. Jones. And before you knew it, they'd told the Chucker about the one-hundred-and-fifty-dollar puppies and Chucker was saying, 'I'm sure there's some mistake. Will you allow me to inquire?' So in he comes, lays one hundred and thirty dollars in my hand with that funny look he sometimes has. Then he goes out and says, 'Just as I suspected. The little boy must have misunderstood the lady. They're only twenty dollars.'

"Well, you know me. I gathered in the twenty dollars and had all I could do not to whimper when those kids took their puppy."

"How'd you move the rest of them?" I asked.

"Spearchucker watched this transaction and he went into what Trapper calls his vaudeville smile, all teeth and whites of eyes, and he says in that fake black routine, 'Miss Lucinda, look like you and me in the puppy business, but first I gotta get us some sustenance.' He reappeared ten minutes later with four sixpacks of Coke and five bottles of what he and Duke call Jack in the Black, Jack Daniels Black Label, and a whole bunch of paper cups and a bag of ice cubes.

" 'Miss Lucinda,' he said, pouring a bourbon and Coke for us, 'we are now in business.'

"You know our office is right on the street. Chucker sipped once on his Jack in the Black and, looking out the window, he says, 'I believe I see a live one.' The live one was Hawkeye Pierce, who was doing his usual last-minute Christmas shopping. As Hawk walked by, the door opened and this great arm just reached out, plucked him off the sidewalk and sat him down on the sofa.

" 'Hey, boy, have a drink,' said Spearchucker.

"You can imagine the conversation, but the end of it was, 'Hawkeye, I Santa Claus. Man, like you gotta tithe for Santa Claus. I'm movin' a few puppies here and I need a contribution of maybe two pneumonectomies from you.'

" 'Christ,' said Hawk, 'that's a large one. A grand even at Blue Shield prices. You're outta your nigger mind.'

" 'Pay, brother. Wasn't that a nice drink?'

"Hawkeye got out his checkbook. 'Who do I make it out to?' he asked.

" 'Santa Claus Jones.'

" 'Okay, buddy boy. You do this to me, you gotta hit some other folks. You want me to steer a few this way?'

" 'Now you talkin', boy. Oops. Wait just a tiny moment.'

"The door opened, the big arm went out and came back in with Dry Hole Pomerleau, the French well-driller. 'Well, lookee here what I found. A rich swamp canary just dying for a drink of good old Jack and a

69

chance to help out Santa Claus.'

" 'What the hell are you up to now, you crazy——?'
Then he stopped, because I was there, but I know what
he was going to say.

" 'I want a check for five hundred bucks so I can play
Santa Claus. That's how much you overcharged me for
that well, because I'm a nigger.'

" 'I didn't overcharge you because you're a nigger, you
goddamn fool. I overcharged you because you're a doctor.'

" 'Five hundred, Dry Hole.'

" 'Do I get a puppy?'

" 'You just get to know that you've made a little kid
happy.'

" 'Okay,' said Dry Hole. 'You get that sonovabitch, Stiff
Standing Hooper, too.'

"At this point," Lucinda told me, "Spearchucker sent
me across the street to cash the two checks. I came back
with fifteen hundred bucks.

" 'What are we doing?' I asked the Chucker.

" 'Well, I'm not sure, but I'm getting a feel for this. We
got the puppies paid for. Let's start giving them away.' "

"It was only ten-thirty. By noon the puppies were
gone and we'd collected another two thousand dollars.
Chucker seemed to have some instinct for matching
puppies and kids. He knew, I'm sure he did, which kid
really wanted a puppy, would love it, care for it, train it.
Three little girls and four more little boys got puppies.
You should have seen the looks, first of wonder, then of
pure joy, when this great black giant came out, spoke to
their parents and got permission for the kid to have a
puppy. Oh, Hook, he was just great."

"You're somewhat partial to superlatives," I reminded

Lucinda, "but okay, he was great. How'd he get the extra two grand?"

"That was just the start of it. Hawkeye and Dry Hole, having been grabbed, steered the suckers in. He got a thousand from my husband by threatening to go to bed with me, and five hundred from Stiff Standing Hooper just by towering over him, and you know how Hooper is with money. About eleven-thirty Crazy Horse Weinstein went by. Well, you know Horse, he's about as big as the Chucker. He was a little hard to drag in. Chucker had to go right out on the street and use two hands. He gave him a drink and said, 'Congratulations, Horse, I'm dealing you in for only five hundred in return for grabbing all the rich Jews for maybe ten grand.'

" 'Who do you think you are?' Crazy Horse demanded.

" 'Man, I Santa Claus.'

"Well, I thought Crazy Horse was going to die laughing, but finally he reached into his pocket and peeled off five hundred-dollar bills. 'Okay,' he said, 'I get you ten grand, we spend it all out on the reservation—food, clothes, toys for kids.'

" 'Deal,' said Chucker. 'Have another Jack in the Black, Horse. How you gonna raise the ten?'

" 'Easy. I'll go to my most prosperous brethren and tell them, for a grand, I can talk you out of moving in next door. Be back in two hours.' "

Lucinda's story was interrupted by an hors d'oeuvre tray and a new drink.

"Well, where was I?" she asked. "Oh, yes. Horse went out to hit half his people so he could play Santa Claus for the other half. There was a lull, so Chucker and I had a drink. It was, I don't know, twelve-thirty, one o'clock, we looked out and we saw Scrooge Prouty coming out of the

71

bank. Scrooge, you know how he walks, like every step might be his last, like a marathon runner the last hundred yards? And he was carrying one of those one quart jars people use to preserve things in, Mason jars, I guess you call them."

Lucinda dissolved into laughter at this point, and the story stopped again, temporarily.

Jim (Scrooge) Prouty, of the Prouty Lumber Company, is a Spruce Harbor Brahmin. Old, old family. His forebears built ships. Much loot. At seventy, Scrooge, a seventeen handicapper, has been through a lot. Hawkeye took out his left lung ten years ago. Spearchucker removed a cervical disc seven years ago. Someone replaced his original right hip joint with a steel prosthesis five years ago. His arthritis is so bad he can't get a golf club back very far. Hawkeye nailed him for a gallbladder just a couple years back and fixed his hernia at the same time. In September of '73, Duke removed his urinary bladder, a cystectomy as my boys say, for cancer. As I understand it, in this kind of case they plug the ureters, the tubes that carry urine from the kidney to the bladder, into an isolated segment of lower small bowel—they call it an ileal bladder. The opening for this is in the right lower quadrant of the abdomen about where many of us have our appendectomy scars. So they'd done this to Scrooge in September. In October Scrooge came back to the hospital with an intestinal obstruction. Duke and Hawkeye operated on him. Where they'd made the new bladder, the small intestine was all stuck down. They freed it up, had to take out about two feet of bowel. For the next two weeks things were nip and tuck, but Scrooge, as usual, emerged victorious and left the hospital in late November. He spent two weeks at home gathering strength before going to the Mid-Ocean Club in Bermuda for sun, golf and assorted rehabilitation. The Bermuda vacation was enjoyable, but toward the end Scrooge wasn't feeling too well. Urine from his new bladder was bloody and foul smelling, and he had a low-grade fever.

For Jim Prouty, the name "Scrooge" is inappropriate, which everybody knows, and which is why, with our simple small-town minds, we think it's funny to call him Scrooge. In some ways he is not loose with his money. Hear him talk, you'd think everybody was out to grab him. "You take that Hawkeye," he'll say, "his wife says she needs a new refrigerator, what's he do? He calls me up, says, " 'Scrooge, I need a thousand, you gotta come in, have an operation.' I says to him, 'Gawd, boy, whyn't you just come down to the yard, hold me up with a gun, take a thousand. I won't have to go through all that sufferin'.' But he says, 'No, Scrooge, I want you to suffer for the refrigerator.' "

Scrooge knows perfectly well that if he went to Boston for his surgery it'd cost him three times as much, and he could afford it, but he keeps on complaining. The thing about Scrooge, though, any time I'm a little short at the hospital and Wooden Leg Wilcox is temporarily embarrassed, Leg'll say, "Call Scrooge, see if he's in a charitable mood." When I call Scrooge, I never get the whining we all hear at the golf course or the Rotary Club. What I hear is, "How much you need, boy?" and "You ain't gonna tell nobody?"

Well, let's get back to the story. Lucinda was telling me about Scrooge coming out of the bank with this jar cradled in his arms. She said Chucker grinned in anticipation, swallowed some Jack in the Black, and put that great black hand on Scrooge as he passed the door.

" 'You leggo me, you darky thief,' Scrooge whined. 'I ain't ready for no more operations.'

" 'I'm Santa Claus,' Chucker explained. 'All I want is a thousand bucks and you don't even have to get operated on. Where else you gonna get a bargain like that?'

" 'Put it that way, I suppose you're right. Not even a hospital bill?'

" 'Straight grand, no strings, Scrooge.'

" 'Mighty nice of you, boy. First time one of you fellers ever let me off so easy. You take my check?'

" 'An honor, Scrooge. May I ask what you have in the jar which you cradle so protectively in your arms like you were carrying it into the Dolphin defense?'

" 'Oh, well, it's sort of a Christmas present for Duke. He made this new bladder for me but it come out. I thought 'twas a mite unusual. Thought he'd like to have it. Don't s'pose I could get my money back.'

"Chucker looked a little alarmed, but not really. 'Now don't you put me on, Scrooge,' he warned. 'You funnin' me, ain't you?'

" 'Hell, no. My bladder, I got it in this here jar.' "

" 'Lemme see,' said Chucker. All of a sudden the game of the day disappeared. Chucker grabbed the jar, took it into the john and poured the contents into the sink. What he saw was about ten inches of necrotic small intestine. He came charging out like he needed two yards to win the Superbowl and ordered, 'Lucinda, find Duke and call the hospital.'

" 'Now you wait just a goddamn minute here, young fella,' Scrooge Prouty whined. 'You told me all I had to do was pay a thousand dollars, I wouldn't have to have

74

no doctors or no hospital. What do you think you're doin' anyhow?'

"There's a sofa in one corner of the office," Lucinda continued. "Chucker picked Scrooge up, laid him down on the sofa and said, 'You just rest easy now, Scrooge baby, we gonna take care of you.'

" 'Here we go again,' moaned Scrooge.

"Duke arrived. He'd already been tapped for a grand and was hanging out in the bank looking for new victims. Spearchucker took him to the john to view the ileal bladder."

Then, as Lucinda told it, "Duke looked like he'd jumped out of his own bladder. He almost ripped Scrooge's clothes off and viewed his belly where the bladder was supposed to empty. 'How you feel, Scrooge?' he asked.

" 'Feel good, Duke. Ever since that thing come out, two weeks ago. Afore that I was feelin' right ghormy.' "

" 'Right what?'

" 'Ghormy.'

" 'Of course. Ghormy. You mean to tell me this happened two weeks ago?'

" 'Ayuh?'

" 'Why the——. I mean why in hell didn't you let me know then?'

" 'I was afeard you'd get all upset.'

" 'I'm all upset now.'

" 'Ayuh, but I tell you, Duke, I thought I was havin' a baby, maybe you fellers knocked me up, when this thing come out. I still got that nice little pink thing on the surface, put the catheter in like you show me, let the water out, feel finestkind. Just was bringin' it in to show you, thought you'd be interested.'

"Hawkeye blew in then and heard the story. 'Jesus,' he said, 'we musta knocked off the blood supply to that christly ileal pouch when we fixed his small bowel obstruction. So, he's leaking urine into a walled-off pocket in his belly instead of the ileal pouch. If he's swinging with it, we sure as hell ain't gonna mess with it.'

"The three doctors," said Lucinda, "mulled this thought for a few seconds, and then Spearchucker said, 'Scrooge, Merry Christmas. Get off the sofa and have some Jack in the Black.'"

Scrooge, liberated, no longer under threat of immediate surgical indictment, moved moderately, as is his way in everything, into the Jack in the Black. Ere long, according to Lucinda McIntyre, he suggested, "If my bladder is as unusual as you fellers seem to think it is, sittin' in that there sink, and you fellers is tryin' to collect money to help the poor folks, which I figure is what's goin' on here, and I gather you run out of puppies, which I gathered before I come, why don't you charge money to look at my bladder? How many of them ileal bladders be they on exhibit for the general public in Spruce Harbor today, or ever in an average ye-ah?"

It was then that Spearchucker sent Lucinda on a special assignment. I've pieced the rest of the story together from further talks with her and others. Everyone agreed that placing Scrooge's bladder on exhibition would, indeed, be a public service. The first customer was Solly (Live Better Electrically) Davis, the new psychiatrist at Spruce Harbor Medical Center. Solly, once of Brooklyn, wore black cowboy boots, Levis, a black leather jacket and a blue button-down Hathaway shirt, all below a big black beard and bright, piercing, sparkling eyes. When

76

Spearchucker saw him coming, he rejoiced.

"Put me down, you meshugene schwartzer," Solly ordered a moment later, "or I'll cool you out with my Thorazine spray gun, in preparation for the electric shock treatments. May I be so bold as to inquire what you and these other Christian gentlemen are doing?"

"For two hundred bucks," Hawkeye exclaimed, "we gonna let you look at Scrooge's bladder."

"It's part of our Christmas pogrom," Scrooge explained.

"I knew it, I knew it," exclaimed Solly. "Everywhere I go, to the school, no matter where, somebody invites me to a Christmas pogrom. I give you two bills, whaddaya do, go buy an oven?"

"We already got the oven. For two bills we won't turn it on."

Solly, he's a little different. He paid the two hundred and joined the group, after politely explaining that, as a psychiatrist, his interest in bladders was minimal.

"Surely," quothe Hawkeye, "someone will wish to view Scrooge's bladder, no doubt a first in urological history. May I have just another small touch of that fine middle-aged mash?"

Chucker, always alert, saw a prominent aviator approach.

"Oh, Lordy, we got us a live one. Here comes The Stoned Eagle, Mr. Wrong Way Napolitano. Yuh all come right in here Wrong Way and have yourself a little warmth."

Whisked off the street, Wrong Way, always a realist, had a drink. "We gotta have two hundred bucks, Wrong Way, or Solly Davis is gonna hit you with his Thorazine spray," he was told.

To reinforce the threat, Solly gave him a small sample of Florient, which Lucinda had used to negate the not inconsiderable smell of Scrooge's bladder.

"Here's the deuce. I better have another drink," said the aviator.

"Finestkind. You wanta see Scrooge's bladder?" offered Solly Davis, who was quick to adopt the native language and custom.

"Sure," said Wrong Way.

"Somebody better go with him" Hawk warned, "make sure he doesn't eat it."

The next victim was the illustrious leader of the Spruce Harbor Mental Health Clinic, Dr. Ferenc Ovari, known to one and all as Rex Eatapuss. Rex, like the others, was speared by the long arm of Spearchucker Jones. His slightly porcine features were reddened and aquiver with fear and noncomprehension when the Chucker placed him on the sofa and said, "Rex, baby, where you been? Ah been waitin' for you. Here, have a nice shot of Jack in the Black."

"I hear you rode into town on a horse with no name," Trapper said to him.

Rex sort of whimpered.

"Two bills for the drink and you get to see Scrooge's bladder," Hawkeye explained.

"Part of our Christmas pogrom," added Scrooge.

"Will you stop saying that?" exclaimed Solly Davis, who approached Rex with his can of Florient and gave him a light dusting. "Two bills, Rex," he repeated, "or I plug you into my electric bed and turn you into a coal miner again."

"Swine," said Rex.

"You're a true con man, Rex," Hawkeye told him.

78

"You talk like a movie hunky. When you were growin' up in Scranton, you'd have said something really unpleasant. Two bills."

Rex paid. The boys forgot to let him see Scrooge's bladder. He left, I guess feeling lucky to escape with his life.

Meanwhile Scrooge, moderately but with the plodding Yankee determination that had characterized his business career, had moved into the Jack in the Black. So determinedly, in fact, that at 2:15 P.M. he said, "I figure this here is a good Christmas pogrom. I gonna match what you get, dollar for dollar."

Hawkeye sat down next to him. "We got thirty-two grand, counting what Crazy Horse'll get from the Hebes. You already gave a grand. Another thirty-one will suffice. Gimme a check. Make it out to Spruce Harbor General."

"I sure as hell ain't gonna make it out to *you.*"

Crazy Horse reappeared with two trucks, ten grand and Tip Toe Tannenbaum. Lucinda McIntyre returned with four social workers, a list of needy families from the County Department of Health and Welfare and two of Scrooge Prouty's lumber trucks.

Lucinda and the social workers spent a hectic hour assessing the needs of various families. By the time they'd made a hasty plan of where and how to spend twenty-one large, Crazy Horse and Tip Toe had already swept through supermarkets buying food, and Zayre's buying clothing and toys for the Indians at Moose Isle Reservation. There are a variety of stories going around about the thirty-mile trip to Moose Isle. It seems that Horse had liberated a bottle of Jack in the Black, fearing a change in the weather. Tip Toe, who does not drink, except when he's driving a truck, is said to have caught the spirit of the season. The only ascertainable fact is that they played Santa Claus at the reservation, where their gifts were received with gratitude. Crazy Horse wants to be governor and, according to Tip Toe, couldn't resist a small political pitch, which prompted one of the Indian leaders to speculate as to whether "Jewboy speak with forked tongue."

Mind you, that's just what Tip Toe told me. I doubt if it's true.

Lucinda organized a twenty-grand food, clothing and toy onslaught for the underprivileged, unfortunate, inept or what have you. She was assisted by my surgeons, the social workers, Solly Davis, Dry Hole Pomerleau and Wrong Way Napolitano. They swept through the stores like a herd of locusts, bringing joy to overstocked proprietors of discount everythings. Darkness was upon them when Lucinda and the social workers embarked in Scrooge's two overloaded trucks, one driven by Hawkeye, the other by the Chucker.

Here and there, isolated farms, walk-up apartments, even a couple of islands visited in Trapper's boat, they appeared, usually led by Spearchucker, who'd announce, "Evenin', I'm with Santa Claus. He told me to leave this stuff here."

By ten o'clock they were done. "You saved out a grand, Lucinda. What's that for?" asked Hawkeye.

"For Pete and Alice. Their puppies got us going, and that'll give them a little extra."

"I suppose that's fair. Horse gave ten grand to the Indians. How about Chucker? Maybe we should have saved something out for the coons."

"Well," said Duke, "don't worry about it. I saw the check he sent to the foundation he and his brothers run in Forrest City, Georgia. That's why he does the work of two neurosurgeons. Half is for him, and half is for something else."

Hawkeye Pierce got home at 11:30 P.M. on Christmas Eve. His wife Mary, a long sufferer who never asks questions, said, "The children missed you."

"I know. I'm sorry. I'll make it up to them tomorrow."

6

MEANSTREAK

JULY 8, 1974.

Last night, in one of the sumptuous function rooms at the Bay View Cafe, three hundred people attended a party for Meanstreak Morse. The headline in today's Spruce Harbor *Gazette* read: "Welcome Home, Meanstreak."

"Probably just got out of jail," I heard a summer complainant say down at the newsstand. That's not the way of it.

Fourteen years ago, in 1960, a short biography of Mr. Morse would have read: "Claremont (AKA Meanstreak, or Mean) Morse. Born March 16, 1923, Crabapple Cove, Maine. Graduated Port Waldo High School 1941 (Allstate center, football). U.S. Marine Corps 1942–1945. Bronze Star. Silver Star. Purple Heart. Married Evelyn Pierce 1941. Five children. Occupation: lobster fisherman; clamdigger. Height 6'4". Weight 230 pounds, all muscle."

Old Mean Morse. I am not usually overly sentimental, but I got all choked up at that party last night. Hawkeye Pierce, Mean and I played on the Port Waldo team that beat Spruce Harbor back in '41. Mean got his name before that. I think it was '39. We were playing Belfast, and Mean was working over their center quite actively. I can still see and hear that kid pointing at Mean, jumping up and down and yelling to one of the officials, "That big sonovahowah Morse has got a mean streak."

In a way, maybe he did, but usually with provocation. When he was seventeen he knocked up Hawkeye Pierce's fifteen-year-old sister Evelyn and had to get married because her father, Big Benjy, was just as big as Mean and came armed to discuss the nuptials. Then there was the war and the Marines and Guadalcanal and Okinawa. Details of all that are hazy. He was, according to the story, recommended for the Congressional Medal of Honor by his commanding officer, who caught a sniper bullet a day later. The recommendation got filed and the witnesses buried. Specifics of his wounds are not known, at least to me. The local consensus at the time was something like, "Jeezely gooks like to shoot the ahss off'n Old Mean."

Mean came home in late '45 for a hero's reception at the Grange Hall in Crabapple Cove. The Spruce Harbor *Gazette* made quite a to-do over him, since he was about the only genuine war hero the area had produced. By this time he and Evelyn had two kids. Mean bought a lobster boat, dug clams, did a little carpentry and other odd jobs, and found time to get three more kids before Evelyn had her hysterectomy. He was a worker, no question about it, made good money for around here, took good care of the kids. Hawkeye's wife Mary got his oldest, Susan, a scholarship into Wellesley, and Mean would go lobstering and dig two tides to keep up with what the scholarship didn't cover.

In 1960 Jocko Allcock and Tip Toe Tannenbaum (the only left-handed Jewish jet pilot, working part-time as the house dick at the Massasoit Inn) went into the insurance business. This was just one of many ventures for these farsighted entrepreneurs, but they pursued it assiduously. Early on they sold Mean Morse a policy designed especially for the self-employed which provided income and vocational retraining in the event of injury at work. Three days later, as Mean bent over to start the day's clam digging, something popped in his back. He collapsed in the mud. Any effort to get up was greeted with muscle spasms so excruciatingly painful that his vocal response attracted the attention of fellow diggers three hundred yards away. Mean was taken to Spruce Harbor Medical Center where Spearchucker Jones sedated him and eventually operated on him for a ruptured intervertebral disc. His recovery was fairly rapid, but he found that he could not dig clams. Spearchucker said that, although the disc problem was solved, Mean had a chronic ligamentous strain induced by bending over the clam hoe from his great height for so many years. Despite Mean's enormous strength, Chucker declared him disabled not only for clam digging but for lobstering, fearing that recurrence of the muscle spasms in a heavy chop five miles offshore might render Mean unable to manage the boat.

So, Jocko and Tip Toe came across with the insurance. Meanstreak Morse, thrity-seven years old, father of five, one kid in Wellesley, another at the University of Maine, was sidelined with an income of one hundred a week. He took to drinking. In the fifteen years since the war, Mean had never been too big on the sauce because there wasn't time for it, but now and then, maybe once a month, he and his father-in-law, Big Benjy Pierce, would get into Benjy's Old Bantam Whiskey. They'd invade the deadfalls and bistros of Spruce Harbor, Maine. After their first invasion, news of their approach caused the Spruce Harbor police force to evacuate any area chosen by the invaders. This was because Meanstreak and Benjy had decided that the police were gooks and Ace Kimball's joint, the Tea House of the March Wind, was Iwo Jima. The devastation wrought upon the police force, to say nothing of the Tea House, has its niche in local history. Mean's overall reputation and Hawkeye's influence with Jocko, Wooden Leg and other czars of Spruce Harbor thwarted any serious attempt at prosecution.

After two months on the Old Bantam, Mean began to taper off, and one day he called upon his insurance agent, Mr. Jocko Allcock, to discuss the vocational retraining clause in the insurance policy. Immediately after Mean's departure, Mr. Allcock headed directly for the Bay View Cafe and started drinking some of Angelo's razor blade soup (Beefeater's on the rocks) and muttering to himself. According to Angelo, asked later to interpret, Jocko muttered consistently and repetitively: "stupid sonovabitch."

After the fourth bowl of razor blade soup, Angelo called Tip Toe Tannenbaum, expressing concern over his partner's future health. Tip Toe was at the airport on his way to Boston, whence he had to drive a 707 to Rome. He suggested consultation with Hawkeye Pierce.

Hawkeye arrived after office hours and joined Jocko. "Whatsa matta, Jock?" he asked. "You seem distraught, perhaps even juiced."

"Your Christless brother-in-law, that's what's the matta."

"What about him?"

"He came in today and wants his insurance to pay for vocational retraining."

"What's wrong with that? It's in the contract, isn't it?"

"Yeah."

"So what are you so upset about? Lord knows, he can't live on a hundred a week, and all he knows is clams and lobsters."

"I'll tell you what's wrong!" roared Jocko. "The stupid sonovabitch wants to be a brain surgeon."

Hawkeye apparently didn't help matters any by relapsing into a seemingly uncontrollable spasm of laughter. This, rather than lulling Mr. Allcock, vexed him to the point of ordering still another bowl of soup. Every time Hawkeye subsided slightly he'd be struck with further spasms. Five minutes passed before the surgeon was able to say, "What the hell are you worried about, Jocko. Even if he had any smarts, Mean couldn't become a brain surgeon. The dumb bastard's only been to high school, he can't even pronounce his own name, he calls himself MO-AHSS and he's thirty-seven years old. Let's see, four years of college, four years medical school, six years of residency. Christ, he'd be fifty-one years old. Impossible, even with the smarts."

"That's what I told him. He picked me up and held me in a corner and said vocational training was due him and he was gonna be a brain surgeon, and me and Tip Toe gotta pay."

"Chrissake, Jocko. Don't worry about it. I'll go talk to him. He'll listen to me."

Later Hawkeye entered his sister's kitchen in the little house near the end of Pierce Road on the shore of Crabapple Cove. "Where's Mean?" he asked.

"Susan is tutoring him. She's home from Wellesley for the weekend."

"Tutoring him in what?"

86

"Spelling."

"Oh, my sweet Jesus," Hawk groaned. "Gimme a drink. I don't suppose you have anything besides that rotgut he and the old man are so thirsty for."

"No, but there's a little left. I'll get it." Pouring her brother a drink, Evelyn Morse said, "He's serious, you know, Hawkeye. You're going to help him."

"Evelyn, honey, don't be ridiculous. Mean's a great guy, the Audie Murphy of Crabapple Cove if you will, but gentle Jesus, he had all he could do to get through high school——"

"You stop, Hawkeye. You're too busy to pay any attention to anybody around here. You don't really know Claremont anymore."

"Claremont? Who the hell is Claremont? Oh, yeah, I forgot."

"Claremont for years has been reading all kinds of books late into the night, then getting up at four-thirty to haul traps. He may not be educated, but he's smarter'n you think and knows more'n you think."

"Come to think of it, that Susan didn't get into Wellesley just on Pierce chromosomes. Maybe I been overlooking something."

"Will you help?"

"Evelyn, please. I'll help, but you have to be realistic. Yes, maybe go to college, be a teacher, maybe coach some football, something like that, but I won't be party to encouraging an impossible dream. It is impossible. You and Mean are a little isolated from the mainstream. You simply have no conception of what you're talking about. As I said, it's ridiculous. I'd be unkind to encourage him."

"Claremont wants to be a brain surgeon. That insurance has to pay, and you're gonna help," Evelyn insisted.

"I doubt like hell the insurance policy covers college expenses. Jocko will try to jink him out of it. Tip Toe Tannenbaum's another story. I probably can get Tip Toe to go along with college. Hell, why not? Let him try college. After a time he'll see for himself the brain surgery bit is foolish, but, like I said, maybe teaching——"

"Thanks, Hawk. You're a great brother."

Hawkeye, picking up the phone, called a familiar number, that of Rat Randall, principal of Port Waldo High and prominent golfer.

"Hey, Rat, I need a favor."

"Yeah. Anything."

"I'm gonna send Meanstreak up in the morning for an IQ test."

"Look, Hawk. Oh well, hell, yes, if you say so."

Mean came out of the back room, the spelling lesson over. Before he could say anything, Hawkeye talked. "Look, Mean, I ain't gonna argue with you. I just called the Rat. He's gonna give you a test in the morning, see if you can get through doors and around corners. Then we'll talk."

Pierce had a call from the Rat the next afternoon.

"Hey, Hawk."

"Yeah."

"I looked up the old records, 1941. He was in two figures. Low normal."

"How'd you clock him today?"

"Two under for 36 at Wawenock (par 70)."

"One thirty-eight?"

"You got it."

"The machinery go haywire? That's about genius country."

88

"Yeah. One of the counselors I got says if he'd been associating with humans instead of Crabapple Cove grunts he might run 150 or better. Seems like he might be intelligent."

"Well, I'll be dipped in lobster bait," said Hawkeye reflectively. "Thanks, Rat."

Dr. Pierce buzzed Alice D'Angelo, his secretary. "Get me the coon," he ordered.

"Do you mean Dr. Jones?"

"You know goddamn well who I mean. You wanta be a Democrat, go on relief."

"I am a Democrat."

"So's the guinea thief you're married to. Get me the coon."

"Yes, sir," with the well-known icicle voice.

When Dr. Jones answered, Hawk asked, "Hey, Chucker, you think Meanstreak could play football for Androscoggin with his back the way it is?"

"You pose a very interesting question," Chucker replied quite delicately. "I have him on back exercises. I know he can't bend over three hours a day on the clam flats, and I don't dare let him be out there all alone hauling traps. On the other hand, he could eat them small college players alive playing center. If he got in trouble, at least there's help nearby, not like he washed up on a ledge cause he couldn't move. I'd say yes, he can try football."

"Good," said Hawkeye.

"You don't seem very surprised."

"I'm surprised at nothing."

Although the time was late to apply for the class of '64 at Androscoggin College, Hawkeye thought he could arrange it. This was because Ho Jon, the Korean houseboy he, Duke and Trapper had sent to Androscoggin nine years earlier, was now the Director of Admissions. Androscoggin College was riding the first ripple of the tide of liberalism that flooded the Sixties. What more appropriate than to make an alumnus who'd arrived the hardest way possible Director of Admissions? Ho Jon, on the job just a year, had ruffled a few alumni feathers by refusing to accept well-financed but poorly endowed alumni offspring. "Time'll come," said Hawkeye, "a nice dumb white Protestant kid won't be able to go to college."

In June 1960 Dr. Pierce called the Director of Admissions and demanded of the secretary. "Lemme talk to the gook. Tell him it's the Hawk."

"Hey, Hawk," he was soon greeted, "how they goin'?"

"Finest kind. Where you been? We ain't seen you."

"Busy keeping people like you out of college. What's up, Hawkeye? You want to get your old man into college?"

"Hey, Babe, nothing like that. I want to do you and Androscoggin a tremendous favor. I want to arrange an interview for probably the greatest scholar-athlete ever attended that college since, maybe, me. He ain't my old man. He's my brother-in-law."

"Oh, come on, Hawk. How old is he?"

"Only thirty-seven. Ho Jon, he fought on Guadal and Oki. Took out yea many Japs."

Hawk figured that might give Mean a little edge. Ho Jon, enlightened as only a young Director of Admissions could be, had never forgotten that his parents and two brothers had been killed by the Japanese. Hawk also figured Ho Jon might turn away even young Pierces

when the time came, but no way he'd turn down Meanstreak Morse.

"He got any brains? He been through high school?"
(We must remember that Ho Jon, although college educated, learned his early English from Hawkeye, Duke
and Trapper John.)

"He graduated high school with me in '41. He just had
an IQ test. He was two under for 36."

"One thirty-eight?"

"Yeah."

"Bring him down."

"Thanks, Ho Jon. Hey, Ho Jon, do it for me once more,
will yuh?"

"What?"

"Say 'cholangiogram.' "

"Chorangiogram."

"Jesus, you're beautiful. I'll see you when?"

"Next Saturday. At 10 A.M."

Hawkeye went down to see Mean Thursday evening
to discuss his forthcoming interview at Androscoggin.
Mean acted a little nervous, so Hawkeye brought in a jug
of gin and produced martinis. Evelyn was even more
nervous, proclaiming that Mean had no clothes fit for a
college interview. Hawkeye insisted that there was nothing to fear, that everyday clothes were fine. He did suggest that Mean refrain from expressions such as, "How
be yuh," and practice saying "yes" instead of "ayuh." He
also explained that although Ho Jon fitted the general
picture of what Mean referred to as a gook, he was a gook
who'd been on our side, and therefore was not to be
annihilated on sight.

"Ayuh," Meanstreak said throughout the visit.

91

On Saturday morning Hawkeye and Mr. Claremont Morse drove down to Androscoggin for a college interview. "Remember, Mean, emphasize the football. What the hell. I been thinking, you got the insurance income, Evelyn'll have to work, but the kids can get scholarships. Maybe you can make a name in football, some medical school will take you on as some kind of late-blooming superachiever."

"Ayuh," said Mean.

The interview, described by Hawkeye that afternoon on the golf course, was interesting.

"I kept telling the big bastard, 'Look, I got this gook in my pocket. Just shut up, speak when spoken to, lay off the grunt jargon you don't know anything else but, there'll be no sweat.'

"So we go into Ho Jon's office and the first thing Mean does is practically crush his hand shaking it and say, 'Hi ya, Ho Jon, how be yuh?' and that christly Ho Jon says, 'Finest kind.' "

"Well," Hawk told us, "from then on I was out of it. Ho Jon had the football coach, what's his name, drop by, he took one look at Mean, he like to send out for a broad and a red convertible. He couldn't do that, but he popped for about a fin a year off the tuition, which is all they can do down there."

That summer Mean and his oldest boy, the one at the University of Maine, set out four hundred traps and hauled them together, both of them earning money for college and this and that. Jocko Allcock was all upset, claiming Mean was supposed to be disabled, but louder voices and stronger forces prevailed. All summer Susan and Claremont, Jr. (for this is his name) spent evenings tutoring their father in everything he'd never learned in

92

high school. Evenings, Mean and his son would jog and work out with a football. They'd take turns centering the ball to Susan or Evelyn, and play man on man. Claremont, Jr., was scheduled to start at fullback for the University that year. Evelyn Morse, who'd been refreshing her typing and accounting skills, was suddenly employed as Spearchucker Jones's personal secretary. So, when September came, Daddy went to Androscoggin, Susan to Wellesley and Claremont to Maine. The three younger kids worked and played until Evelyn got home at night.

Nobody saw much of Meanstreak Morse that fall. Word from Ho Jon was that he studied all the time, and of course there was football, so he didn't get home weekends, except an occasional Sunday.

Football was not big at Androscoggin in those days, although backalong they'd been competitive with the Little Ivies, Amherst, Williams and Wesleyan. The '60 season was a turnabout for the Black Knights of the Androscoggin. They came into the final game against the University of Maine undefeated. The winner would win "The Maine Series," not earthshaking south of Kittery but very important here. Overall, the Androscoggins had a fair team, but their strength was their defense. At a time when two-platoon football hadn't reached Down East, the name of the defense was the Androscoggin center, and linebacker, Meanstreak Morse. Despite his age, he could still move in spurts, he'd been physical all his life and he was playing against kids much smaller and nowhere near as tough.

On the eve of the Maine-Androscoggin game, Hawkeye and I and Wooden Leg, Me Lay Marston, Jocko Allcock and others who'd played with or against Mean back in high school all went down to Androscoggin with our wives. Evelyn and the other kids came along. Susan came up from Wellesley. Mean had dinner with us at the Stowe House. Everyone except Mean, even his wife, had a few pops of this or that. After Evelyn's third drink (a personal record for her, her brother assured me) she brought up an issue that had been widely discussed in the newspapers but one none of us had wanted to mention.

Down at the State University in Orono, most of the ink had been going to the exploits of the sensational sophomore fullback, Claremont Morse, Jr., who'd averaged 150 yards rushing and had already broken all-time records. "Big, tough, aggressive," the papers said. "Great second effort. Smart, 6'2", 215, and still growing."

Into her third drink, in the dining room of the Stowe House, Evelyn Morse made her pronouncement, "Mean Morse, you listen to me. You hurt one hair of that child's head, don't you ever bother to come home. I'll never speak to you again."

No one laughed, at least aloud. Mean assured his wife that all would be well, then returned to his dormitory. The next day is history. Androscoggin 3; Maine 0. There was a picture in the Sunday *Telegram* showing Claremont Morse, Jr., pointing a finger at his father and remonstrating with one of the zebras. We were all certain that what Claremont was saying was, "That sonovahowah Morse has got a mean streak."

Maybe not a mean streak. But whatever it was that carried Mean through the South Pacific, winning medals, came out that afternoon. He was all over the place, and the little fellows on that Maine team couldn't protect their fullback from his father. Mean racked Claremont up at the Androscoggin 3 on the last play of the game. Before they got up he said, "Hey, boy, you want a be-ah."

"I sure do and you're buyin', you mean old sonovabitch."

Several of us waited outside the Androscoggin locker room while Mean showered. Jocko and Wooden Leg picked up Claremont and we all went to the Alumni House for the usual postgame talk and booze. As Mean walked in I noticed he was limping a little, but he didn't seem to be in any great pain. He greeted Claremont and said, "Boy, we gonna have a few. Dry too long." And they did. Evelyn, wife and mother, watched anxiously. Every now and then, despite growing anesthesia, she saw Mean wince and grimace in discomfort, if not pain. She found her employer and said, "Dr. Jones, will you keep an eye on Mean? I think he's hurt."

Mean and Claremont came home later that evening, both of them somewhat obtunded. Evelyn drove. "We're home," she announced to her sleeping beauties as she moored the pickup truck in the Morse front yard. Young Claremont rolled out first, but Mean, sitting in the middle, just grunted. "What's wrong?" asked his son.

"I can't move. Back's gone again, Ev, honey, bring me my medicine."

Evelyn knew from previous experience the medicine required to get Mean out of the pickup. He needed a tall glass of Old Bantam, three ice cubes and three aspirin. She disapproved of this therapy, but what could she do? Fifteen minutes later, the Old Bantam and the aspirin working, Meanstreak crawled out of the cab, painfully waddled into the kitchen, refilled his glass and struggled to his bed. Evelyn and Claremont helped

95

him undress and tucked him in.

"Serves you right, you mean old bastard," his son said, instead of, "Good night, Daddy."

In the morning Evelyn summoned Dr. Jones, who dropped by after golf to say, "Mean, you're scratched. Your football career is over. You'll get over this, but another season and you might wind up with some permanent damage. It's not worth it."

"Suits me," Mean grunted. "I had alla this I need. Me'n the boys gotta haul traps next summer, pay for all the educations. Guess I'll save myself for that."

In early December of '61 the name Morse appeared prominently in the papers. Mean and Claremont, Jr., both received honorable mention for Little All-American. Mean finished just behind his son in the annual vote for "Maine's outstanding scholar-athlete." This involved a banquet and, according to Hawkeye, "entirely too much publicity, because all they do is harp on how old he is. When we try to get him into med school, that ain't gonna help us any."

Relieved of athletic responsibility, Mean Morse hit the books harder than ever. Each summer he and the boys hauled four hundred traps. Despite the "disability" declared by Spearchucker, no one seemed to object. Economically, what with bright kids getting scholarships and Evelyn working, the Morses were better off than ever. Of course, Mean still had his bill a week from the insurance company.

In May of Mean's junior year, Ho Jon came down to Wawenock to play golf with his old friends from the 4077th MASH. This was always a tense time. Ho Jon had first hit a golf ball with an old 8-iron Hawkeye brought to Korea. Twelve years later, he'd learned how to use

96

other clubs and had a strong four handicap. Hawkeye, Duke, Trapper and Spearchucker varied from sixes to nines, but more often than not blew into the middle 80's. Ho Jon's visits to Wawenock invariably enriched him and caused Trapper John to characterize him as "probably the foremost Korean golf hustler in the Pine Tree State."

"So what's new?" Hawkeye asked the guest over gin and tonic in the locker room after the game.

"You wish news of Meanstreak?" Ho Jon asked.

"If you insist."

"I got good news and bad news. Which you wanna hear first?"

"The good news, I guess," said Spearchucker.

"He made Junior Phi Bete."

"I'll be double dipped," marveled Hawkeye, who informed the group that he, while at Androscoggin, hadn't come within sight of this signal honor.

There were so many exclamations of wonder and joy that Ho Jon had to remind his companions that there was bad news.

"What?" asked Trapper.

"Two nights ago he went to a party given by the Political Science Department. He got mad and beat up the whole department."

"What's so bad about that?" Hawk asked. "They're just a bunch of lefties, aren't they? Good for them. Fella oughta kick the bejusus out of a liberal now and then just to stay in shape."

"Only two things you can do with those folks," Trapper said, "beat 'em up or raise their salaries and make 'em conservatives. Truly a delicate balance."

"What's gonna happen?" Dr. Jones asked.

97

"They're trying to get him thrown out."

"What the hell happened, anyway?"

"Well," said Ho Jon, "it seemed that there was talk of Yankee Imperialism, of interference with the progress of Communism in Korea, Southeast Asia, Eastern Europe and Africa. At least this is how Meanstreak seemed to take it. What he told me was, 'I felt constrained, as a loyal American and a former member of the U.S. Marines, to kick the bejesus out of these puny little closet commies.'"

"That's what college can do for a man," Dr. Jones observed. "Three years ago he never would have 'felt constrained.'"

"Mean really had no choice, under the circumstances, did he?" asked Hawkeye, impaling Ho Jon on a hostile, determined glare.

"He coulda just gone home, couldn't he?"

"Not a man of honor like Meanstreak Morse. Whadda we gotta do to get him off the hook?"

"Probably nothing. I've already called every alumnus I know who makes over fifty grand a year. Calls already coming in."

"That's good. Mean hurt anybody?"

"He didn't leave any marks but he may have scarred their psyches some."

"Good man, Meanstreak," Hawkeye said. "Guess we'll have to get him into medical school after all."

"That won't be too easy," Ho Jon worried. "I've been sounding out a few places. They like his marks and leadership and football background, but when they hear he's forty years old, they take the choke."

"We'll have to mull that one," Trapper thought aloud.

Getting into medical school has always been difficult. In the mid '60's, because the world of physics and electronics attracted a high percentage of the brightest kids, the squeeze wasn't as tight as it is now. Still, the competition was relatively fierce. By the fall of '64 the Men of the Swamp and their protégé, Ho Jon, realized they had a problem. Incidentally, Claremont, Jr., was already at the University of Vermont School of Medicine where they almost threw him out for declaring that Mean was his brother instead of his father.

Ho Jon came down one bleak November Wednesday (no good for golf) for a council of war and lunch at the Bay View.

"We've gotta come up with something," he told the four Swampmen. "They just won't take a forty-year-old man anymore. They say by the time he graduates he'll have less than half a career ahead of him and it's not fair to the younger applicants."

Hawkeye arrived late. He'd just returned from a course in vascular surgery at the Mid-State Medical Center somewhere in New York. He was brought up-to-date on the Mean Morse situation. He brooded, thought, ordered a mart and yelled at Angelo, "Hey, Angelo, is Tip Toe in town?"

"Yeah."

"Call him. Tell him to get down here."

"What's up?" Trapper asked.

"I got a secret. I met the Dean of this Mid-State Medical Center and College of Medicine, strictly a Hebe outfit. Dean's name's Tannenbaum. I asked was his brother an airplane pilot, he said yes."

"Ah, so," from Ho Jon.

"Just what do you have in mind?"

Hawkeye asked, "Would you guys kick in a grand a year to help Mean through school? We could deduct it, some way, with the help of a crook lawyer. Say we let Tip Toe and Jocko off the hook for vocational retraining if Tip Toe leans on his brother to take Mean in medical school. We give him four grand a year. He's got a fin from his disability, Evelyn's working, the kids all work and get scholarships. Nobody gets hurt."

Captain Irving Tannenbaum, Chief Pilot of Intercontinental Airways, entered the Bay View warily, forewarned by Angelo that something was in the wind. He was greeted effusively and given a comfortable chair next to the fireplace in Angelo's new cocktail lounge. A large bloody Mary with celery and meatball was placed before him.

"Great to see you, Toe," Trapper greeted him.

"Sure glad yuh all could join us," said Duke.

"Always a pleasure, Captain," Hawkeye agreed.

Tip Toe beckoned to Angelo, who came over. "Angelo," he asked, "what do you think I should do?"

"Cut out. They settin' you up for somethin'."

"Gentlemen," Tip Toe addressed his friends, "the answer obviously is no, but satisfy my curiosity. What's the question."

"Tip Toe, you are aware of the ambitions of your client, Mr. Meanstreak Morse, are you not?"

"Am I ever," the pilot groaned.

"We gonna lift a great burden from your shoulders. We are gonna rescue the Allcock-Tannenbaum Insurance Company, somewhat," Spearchucker told him.

"Oh? What do I have to do? Smuggle heroin?"

"No," said Hawkeye. "Now look, Toe, don't snow us. I met your brother, the head Hebe at Mid-State Medical. All you gotta do is call him, tell him take Meanstreak, we'll pay the tuition. You won't have to."

"Angelo," commanded the pilot, "bring me your phone."

Tip Toe called his brother, person-to-person, collect, and the conversation went like this:

"Izzy, how are you? This is your brother the pilot.

"Finestkind. Say, Izzy, you and Sarah still flying to Tel Aviv next month?

"Good. I made all the arrangements. My company. Won't cost you a cent.

"You're welcome, Iz. I know you'll enjoy. By the way, Izzy, I want to thank you in advance for accepting a young friend of mine in your medical school.

"Why, no, he hasn't applied. We can take care of the formalities later. Kindly send a letter of acceptance to Mr. Meyer Morse, Crabapple Cove, Maine. No fear. Junior Phi Beta Kappa. Little All-American, football. Nice Jewish boy.

"How the hell do I know what it was before he changed it to Morse? Does it matter?"

"He's only forty, maybe forty-one.

"Izzy. They're giving me a bad time about you and Sarah. Tel Aviv, Rome, last year New Zealand, all free. You owe me.

"Same to you, Izzy.

"Of course I'm sure he's Jewish. Why is it so important? You already filled the goy quota?

"I see. Well, then, he'll have to be Jewish, won't he?

"Thanks, Izzy. Say hello to the family. Nice talking to you."

Replacing the phone, Tip Toe grinned in triumph. "Nothing to it, gentlemen. Furthermore, Allcock and Tannenbaum meet their obligations. You folks won't have to ante up."

"Tip Toe," said Hawkeye, "you're a jewel."

"But a good guy just the same," observed Trapper.

"I said 'jewel,' you putz."

"Oh."

Spearchucker, obviously puzzled, said, "This here's all mighty fine, Toe, but there's this little bit about Meanstreak being Jewish."

"That is a problem. Izzy says it'll be easier, all things considered, if he comes on Jewish. Already over the Christian quota. Said he could use a couple gooks, but I think Mean is more Jewish than Oriental, wouldn't you agree, Ho Jon?"

"Most assuredry. Mean has had a Jewish roommate for the last two years. He won't have any trouble passing."

"Yuh all gonna have to circumcise him so's he can pass the physical exam," Duke told them.

"Oh, come on, let's not overdo it, said Hawkeye. "He can just say the *mohel* blew it, well, missed the cut, whatever."

"Circumcise him, have him grow a beard," advised Tip Toe. "He could win mayor in Tel Aviv."

"I don't like it," groaned Hawkeye.

"Why not?"

"Well, it just doesn't set right with me. Mean has earned a chance. Why should he have to sail under a different flag? It'll be hard to explain to him and Evelyn, the whole family."

"A month ago," Dr. Jones reminded Hawkeye, "you were all for dipping him in chocolate and sending him to Meharry."

"I was just talkin'."

"There's nothing dishonest about it," Tip Toe explained. "It'll just save Izzy a bit of embarrassment. He can justify admitting a forty-one-year-old man if a story goes with it. It's just that Mean's real story is not a winner at Mid-State Medical. If I know Izzy, he'll come up with a story."

The phone rang. "For you, Toe," said Angelo.

"Izzy? Yeah. What's up?

"I was just saying, if I know you, you'd come up with a story, but really, Iz, I don't know if I can get this guy to hold still for tattoos.

"If you say so, Izzy. I'll see what I can do. So long."

The pilot faced the group. "Izzy says Meyer Morse has to have some numbers tattooed on his left forearm. Seems they have an opening for a kid who prepped at Auschwitz."

"Oh, my holy, bleeding Christ," groaned Dr. Pierce. "There's only one way, I suspect, that Mean'll buy this. You guys don't know him as well as I do. He does not have a devious bone in his body, like all us sophisticated folk."

"Whadda ya mean?"

"He's gotta join the Hebe church for real. That way it'll be on the up and up. I suppose he'll hold still for the tattoo. As a result of World War II, although his attitude toward the Japanese remains antagonistic, he also hates Krauts."

"I may have to move out of Crabapple Cove," said Duke. "Don't believe I'd care to live in a Jewish neighborhood."

Mean came home the weekend after Wednesday's working lunch. All charges against him had long since been dropped by the Political Scientists. Alumni pressure had threatened them with a financial quandary that could serve only to increase their liberalism, so their

103

conservatism took over. Ho Jon had spent two long nights convincing Mean that his conversion to Judaism was reasonable and justified. Ho Jon went over Mean's application to Mid-State Medical (Izzy sent it special delivery) very carefully, changing only the religious question. Mean had written "Hebe," but Ho Jon changed it to "Jewish." The application went into Saturday morning's mail.

Within a few days Claremont (Meanstreak) Meyer Morse had been circumcised by Duke, tattooed by a minion of Wooden Leg Wilcox and, under the auspices of Tip Toe, begun his conversion. Every effort was made to keep all this quiet, but nothing is quiet for long in places like Spruce Harbor and Crabapple Cove. Early on there was talk, some needling, some laughter. Hawkeye predicted that there'd be no major problem, theorizing that 6'4", 230-pound Hebes are seldom afflicted with overt anti-Semitism. As the summer progressed, Mean Morse was deeper and deeper into his new religion, declaring that he found it much more stimulating spiritually and intellectually than the Nazarenes, the Witnesses, the Spirits, the Full Gospels or the Bible Baptists, and he said, "The preacher feller, whatcha call him, the Rabbi, the sonovabitch even reads books."

There was a suggestion that Mean, to maintain his new image at the Mid-State Medical College, should learn Yiddish. Tip Toe voted this down, pointing out that, despite the Phi Bete key, Mean's English was still primordial. Tip Toe suggested that Mean's best bet, for the first few months in medical school, was to say as little as possible in any language.

Mean grew a bushy black beard in preparation for his new membership in the Jewish quota at Mid-State. Once he got there, he worked hard and said little. He was an object of wonder and awe to his younger classmates. Also, one gathers, fear. A month after starting medical school Mean broke up an anti-Vietnam demonstration that he felt was interfering with his educational program. He broke it up by picking up a "Puny little pink ass" in each huge paw and carrying them to the laboratory where they were supposed to be. After a few trips, the others figured they'd better get back to work.

After a couple of years at Mid-State, according to news leaked Down East by Dean Izzy Tannenbaum, there was some doubt as to exactly who was running the outfit, him or Meanstreak Morse. "It's okay, though," Izzy said. "At least we don't have any student demonstrations because Mean doesn't hold with demonstrations."

Eventually, Izzy revealed, some of the students had reason to doubt Mean's ethnic and other backgrounds. This was partly a result of interclass basketball games in which Mean demonstrated techniques virtually unknown to survivors of concentration camps. Probably the biannual visits of Mean's father-in-law, Big Benjy Pierce, did a lot to destroy Mean's credibility. Benjy, now and then, drives a load of lobsters to New York for Wooden Leg Wilcox. On these occasions he'd stop in to see Mean on the way home, parking the lobster truck in the student parking lot. On these occasions Mean would interrupt his strict work program and get drunk with his father-in-law. After a few pops, the relatives usually decided that a program of ideological revision should suddenly be added to the medical school curriculum. The program invariably began with Mean's proclamation: "Let us proceed to the Student Union and discuss life with some draft dodgers."

Even with his beard, even adorned in conservative non-clam-digging threads, Mean Morse still looked like a drill sergeant on pass from Camp Lejeune. After Benjy's third visit, Dean Tannenbaum called Tip Toe. The Dean was disturbed.

"Look, Irving," he said to Tip Toe, "you gotta do something about that animal who comes down from Maine and gets Meyer Morse all worked up. You wanna know what they did this time?"

"No," said Tip Toe.

"They shanghaied six of my kids into the Marines."

"Oh, come, Izzy. How could they do that?"

"They brought a bunch of Marine recruiters right into the Student Union and made the kids sign up, that's how they could do it. Pure intimidation."

"Oh, come on. Just the two of them couldn't intimidate a whole medical school."

"They had help. I got two black kids, fought in Nam. Your guys got them juiced, too. I figure Mean, Benjy, those two schwarzers could beat up the whole school. Some of my kids aren't what you'd call physical."

"One would certainly have to classify such behavior as slightly reprehensible," Tip Toe agreed.

"Slightly! You meshuganeh! Why just slightly?"

"Well, really, Izzy, if they'd tried harder they could easily have gotten more than six, wouldn't you say? So what happened? The Marines keep 'em?"

"Hell, no. They examined them and found them unworthy or something."

"So, what's your beef?"

"I can't have it. I don't mind Mean keeping this bunch from going crazy, but he comes on like the SS. He doesn't watch out, he's gonna be out, and me with him."

"I'll speak to Benjy," Tip Toe assured his brother.

This episode took place just before Thanksgiving, Mean's second year at medical school. After recruiting the six tigers for the Marines, Benjy, Mean and the black medical students all piled into the lobster truck and headed for a long weekend in Crabapple Cove. They got in late Wednesday afternoon. News of their exploit had preceded them. Evelyn received her husband and her father quite coolly, but was charmingly hospitable to the two medical students who weren't quite sure where they were or how they got there.

"These men are ex-Marines," Mean told Evelyn, "and they are in my class and they're the only white, er, uh, I mean, they're about the only guys, well, hell, honey, you know what I mean."

Hawkeye dropped in to invite the Morses and their guests for Thanksgiving dinner at his house.

Hawk mixed a drink and, before he could be introduced, he said to the two strangers, "Welcome, gentlemen. I see Mean brought two other Jew boys with him."

"Don't mind him, fellas," Mean ordered. "He's a bigot."

"Good," said Jack Andrews, the larger of the ex-Marines (he's doing urology down Belfast way now). "I guess we are, too. Our classmates sure as hell think so."

Thanksgiving was a success that year. The ex-Marines initial impression of Crabapple Cove was that they wished they were back on the Mekong Delta, but the Cove grew on them. Spearchucker came down to meet them, and I guess that impressed them some.

Back at school, Meanstreak, perhaps to save his own skin, became less militant and more tolerant. When Big Benjy visited they just had a few pops with the ex-

107

Marines and attempted no ideological revisions. During his senior year Mean was selected, for three months, to go to the University of Tel Aviv as an exchange student. This was despite the fact that his bogus background had long since been exposed. Evelyn went with him, and I guess they had quite a time.

We all went to work to get Meanstreak an internship down at Maine Medical Center in Portland. That was no problem, and he stayed there for his neurosurgical residency.

As I said backalong, there was a big party at the Bay View Cafe last night. Mean had to give a little speech. He particularly thanked the Allcock-Tannenbaum insurance agency for subsidizing his education.

At the end of the party, Dr. Jones was also asked to speak. "I can't tell you how proud my partner and I are to welcome Dr. Morse to our neuro-surgical group," etc. He concluded with, "As you know, I have resigned as chief of our department of Neurological Surgery, and Claremont Morse, Jr., who joined us last year, has assumed my administrative responsibilities. I will ask Dr. Morse to say a few words, and then we'll all go home."

The Chief of Neurological Surgery, now 6'5" and 235 pounds, ascended the podium and said, "I just want to say this. I'm gonna run a real tight neurosurgical service, and I can take you now, you mean old bastard."

7

THE MOOSE OF MOOSE BEND

ONE of my recurring administrative headaches for over ten years has been that, in the Spruce Harbor Medical Center's operating suite, Duke Forrest and his patients get preferential treatment. Hawkeye, Trapper and Spearchucker get taken care of pretty well, but Duke is The Man. Duke wants to schedule something, everybody gets swept aside. Not a week goes by that someone, usually a tonsil jerker, an orthopod or a cataract plucker doesn't storm into my office, swearing vengeance against Duke and whatever it is that makes him The Man.

The explanation begins in 1951, when Laurier Castonguay of Moose Bend, Maine, was drafted by the Army of the U.S. This was a broadening experience for a young Canuck whose previous travels had been north to Jackman and south to the Skowhegan jail. He was not a criminal, but Laurier Castonguay was this kind of guy: you took one look at him and you knew he should be in jail. His criminal activities did not exceed deer jacking, drunkenness, sexual promiscuity and the simple fact of being a Castonguay from Moose Bend where everybody is named Castonguay. There are a number of reasons why they'd all be Castonguays even if they weren't all named Castonguay, but in the final analysis they are all named Castonguay because it's easy that way and the easy way is the best way in Moose Bend.

The Army, in its infinite wisdom, evaluated Laurier Castonguay and concluded that he should join the infantry. After all, he'd grown up with a rifle in one hand and a jacklight in the other. In Korea he was told that the technique of Chink catching differed in certain ways from deer jacking. He probably didn't understand what they were saying, and if he had he wouldn't have believed them. A jacklighter, one way or another, he skylined himself one evening as the sun sank into the Yellow Sea, popped a Lucky into his mouth, happily thumbed his Zippo into flame and leisurely lit the Lucky. Before he shut the Zippo, a benevolent Chinese provided him with the million dollar wound: a through-and-through perforation of the left chest without apparent damage to any vital structure except lung, which can often take care of itself. He got a Purple Heart and a ticket home.

The trip home for Laurier Castonguay was hurried at first but became leisurely later on. In early darkness he was transported to the 4077th Mobile Army Surgical Hospital by a chopper pilot with more guts than brains. He flew at night because the doctor in the Battalion Aid Station thought the jacklighter might not last till morning. At the MASH a surgeon put a tube in Laurier's chest to drain out blood and gave him three pints of blood; he survived without major surgery. From the 4077th, our hero was evacuated to Yong-Dong-Po and then to a hospital in Osaka, Japan. Private Castonguay, although he recovered rapidly, did not return to combat. This was not because the Army determined that he lacked talent for combat. The Army, in its infinite wisdom, just de-

110

cided to reassign him in Japan.

Japan was a place where even Laurier Castonguay of Moose Bend, Maine, could go good, and he did. He found a moose. The word "moose" meant girl, more or less, at that time, in that place. Her name was Amiko. Private Castonguay, after shacking up with Amiko for a week, offered marriage. This was the dream of the moose herd, which knew that all Americans are rich. Amiko, Private Castonguay and their son, Jacque, arrived in Moose Bend a year later. Amiko looked for the milk and the honey, but all she saw were empty beer cans and Castonguays. Laurier taught her very little English because his native tongue is pidgin French. Amiko was not at a loss, however, because she'd learned one invaluable speech: "Gimme pound of hot dog." The hot dogs, supplemented by trout and venison, allowed her to feed her family, which increased to four by 1957.

Over the years Amiko decided that as things go in Moose Bend, or maybe the world, she wasn't too badly off. She had the Oriental philosophy and rolled with the punches. This was a useful attitude. Laurier got drunk every Saturday night and beat hell out of her. Then he'd push her into bed, jump on, roll over shortly thereafter and fall sound asleep.

In January 1957 Amiko discovered a swelling in her neck. She became more dyspneic than usual while submitting to her hero's athletic feats. In May she mentioned this to him and was appropriately rewarded. By July, however, Laurier became annoyed because Amiko was having trouble transporting the hot dogs, so he took her down river to a quack who knew there was no money in neck lumps from Moose Bend. He accepted five bucks for twenty pink aspirins and wished her well.

111

In October Amiko was brought by ambulance to Spruce Harbor. She was admitted to the hospital and assigned to Duke Forrest, the surgeon on call. A biopsy established the diagnosis of adenocarcinoma of the thyroid gland. The pathologist couldn't define the degree of malignancy, but there was no doubt that the tumor was big and very much in the way. She could neither breathe nor swallow normally. Duke scheduled her for surgery two days later, but this was a day too late. The night before surgery Mrs. Castonguay became cyanotic, and unconscious. She could not breathe at all.

When Duke arrived a tracheostomy set was ready, but there was no time to move her to the operating room. She was in a dark alcove because the hospital was too full. She needed a tracheostomy right then and there—not a few minutes later—if she were to have any chance at all. Duke grabbed a pair of gloves and a scalpel, wondering how he was going to find the displaced trachea in the dark with that big tumor surrounding it. Fumbling his way with no good help and no good light, he cut an internal jugular vein. Blood flowed out of the wound and down over Amiko's bare chest like lava from an erupting volcano. Duke swore, stuffed in a sponge and told a nurse to lean on it while he fixed the windpipe between his fingers, stabbed it and forcefully shoved in a trach tube.

He ordered one nurse to keep pressure on the vein and another to administer oxygen while he ran to the blood bank, found a pint of type O blood, ran back, cut down on a vein in the right groin and started the blood without bothering to cross match it. A lab technician arrived to prepare more blood. The slit in the jugular vein sealed itself off, but Amiko was unconscious with little blood pressure and no palpable pulse. Leaving or-

112

ders to push the blood, Duke slept in the recovery room, figuring the cause was lost and the transfusions were gestures to his conscience.

He awoke at 7 A.M., surprised at having slept so long and sure that Amiko had died. He walked to the surgical ward, his mind on other patients. A glance at the cul-de-sac in the hallway established Amiko's absence. The head nurse said, "Good morning, Doctor. We moved Amiko into 207."

"Whadda you mean? You mean she's okay?"

"You come with me."

He followed the nurse into 207. She stopped, turned and smiled in triumph. Amiko looked up from breakfast with a big grin and held out her hand. Duke took it. She held on for a good thirty seconds, just looking at him. Then, with a shy smile, she said, "Thank you."

Duke stood there looking foolish while Amiko sipped her tea.

"Her breathing is fine," said the nurse, "and she seems to swallow much better since you did the tracheostomy."

"How come you gave her breakfast? I got her scheduled for surgery."

"I thought you'd want to wait."

"You're right, of course. Excuse me. I'm so surprised I can't think."

Amiko smiled at him again and pointed to her neck.

"You fix," she said. It wasn't a question. It was a statement of total confidence in Duke's ability "to fix."

"You goddamn well better believe it," Duke said and meant it, emotionally, but he knew that surgical triumphs aren't achieved at the emotional level and wondered about himself. Still, this was language Amiko understood. She finished breakfast, confident of the future.

Three days later surgery involved an extensive bilateral neck dissection plus splitting the sternum and scooping out tumor that surrounded the trachea all the way down to where it divides. A lot of tumor was left behind, but Amiko's neck had its normal contour, and pressure on the trachea and esophagus had been relieved.

Amiko thought she was cured and that Dr. Duke was Jesus Christ, Buddha, Emperor Hirohito and Elvis Presley all wrapped up in one package. Effective communication with her was impossible, and she was the only one around who thought Duke was that great, so he accepted her evaluation. He started her on thyroid hormone, which occasionally will help her kind of cancer—and it helped hers. In a few weeks she was miraculously cured.

This miracle didn't impress Amiko as much as it did Duke because she expected it. When Duke made rounds she greeted him with a foolish grin, which he chose to interpret as blind adoration. Whatever he said made her smile from ear to ear, and Amiko's face is so arranged that she can nearly do it.

Information provided by nurses and other sources allowed Duke to reconstruct Amiko's past and assess part of her future. The latter was easy. She'd go home and cheerfully submit to the whims, fancies and muscles of Moose Bend's only war hero. Laurier Castonguay was impatient throughout his wife's hospitalization. He wanted her home because he was tired of the kids, and a man from Moose Bend doesn't like to cook his own hot dogs. His visits, though infrequent, upset her. He came only to demand that she return home immediately.

Two weeks after surgery the head nurse called Duke and said Mr. Castonguay was on the ward, trying to cause trouble. Duke went to the ward and invited Mr. Caston-

114

guay to join him in the doctors' room for a quiet conversation.

"Sit down," he suggested, because Mr. Castonguay just stood in front of him and glared.

"By Jeez, when you gon sen Miko home, you?" he demanded.

"Laurier," Duke said, "I know you don't understand much English, but I'm going to speak very slowly. You pay attention, and I think you'll be able to understand me."

"By Jeez," Laurier said, starting another speech, but Duke shoved him into a chair and continued. "Sit down and keep your mouth shut, you stupid sonovabitch."

Mr. Castonguay sat down.

"I'm going to send Amiko home in a week," Duke said. "I shall expect to see her every two weeks here in the clinic. Every time she comes here I'm going to find out if you've been good to her. If I ever hear of you beating her up, I'm not going to call the cops. I'm coming to Moose Bend, and when I leave there's going to be a dead Frenchman, and the dead Frenchman is going to be you. Any questions?"

Amiko returned every two weeks for a while but then stopped coming, and Duke lost track of her. He didn't forget her, but doctors get busy with new patients and one can do just so much. Six months after surgery Duke insisted that she be contacted. A visiting nurse went to Moose Bend and reported that Amiko "seemed to be all right."

In May 1959, a year after Amiko's discharge, Duke, Trapper John, Hawkeye and Spearchucker decided to take advantage of Doggy Moore's offer to use his camp on an island in Lake Chesuncook in northern Maine.

115

This is an area of relative wilderness where paper companies own all the land and where the fishing, in May, is good, and the blackflies would eat an elephant, tusks and all. The four surgeons boarded Hawkeye's station wagon on Saturday morning with hope, enthusiasm, beer, booze, food and a variety of fishing equipment. The road to Chesuncook goes through Moose Bend, so Duke decided to make a house call on Amiko Castonguay. Moose Bend offers the weary traveler a store that sells beer and groceries, and a sleazy restaurant where woodsmen eat venisonburgers and drink beer. There are some rickety trailers, a few tar paper shacks and a haphazard blend of empty beer cans and Castonguays. The fishermen asked for Amiko at the store and were directed to a tar paper shack that sat precariously on the edge of a rushing stream, along with an outdoor privy. The front yard was a sea of mud which, unfortunately, was not deep enough to engulf the rusted carcass of a 1951 Kaiser that sat smack-dab in its middle. In 1951 someone said that the Kaiser, if it had been called a Buick, would have sold like hotcakes. In 1959 a new Silver Cloud wouldn't have looked good in this location, particularly with two frail chickens and a depleted tomcat perched on its roof.

"Looks like a nigger shack down home," said Duke.

"Down home," said Spearchucker, "no niggers live this way. Only poor white trash."

"You guys wait," ordered Duke. "Ah'm goin' in."

Duke couldn't knock on the door because it was open, as were the windows, which had no screens. Duke found Amiko changing diapers on the latest dividend of Laurier Castonguay's Saturday night beer and whiskey libido. When she saw Duke standing there, taking in her scene, Amiko was, of course, surprised. Overcoming this, she was ashamed, but her pride was strong so she smiled. Her smile was not the ear-to-ear phenomenon she'd given Duke the morning after he'd saved her life. It was a tentative, confused smile.

Duke assessed his patient and decided that her emaciation was more likely due to malnutrition than recurrence of thyroid cancer. The children, who played listlessly in one corner, the chickens and the tomcat obviously shared the deprivation.

"Doctor Duke," said Amiko, "why you come here?"

"Amiko, I should have come sooner."

"What you mean, Doctor Duke?"

"Honey, all you and I went through, it turns out I've let you down. This is no way for you to live. Where's that no-good husband of yours?"

"To restaurant."

Duke turned and started to leave, with just one thought. He was going to the so-called restaurant and beat hell out of Laurier Castonguay. Amiko knew this and ran to him and took his arm.

"Please, Doctor Duke," she begged, "don't hurt him. He good to me, now, since you talk to him. It's just Laurier, he no good. He no know how to do nothing. Laurier, you think I crazy, I love him."

Duke tried to comprehend, decided he couldn't and walked out saying: "I'm going to the store and get something for you and the kids to eat."

Outside in the station wagon, the surgical talent, under the influence of Moose Bend, had opened cans of beer. They saw Duke stalk out of Amiko's shack and head for the grocery store. Ten minutes later he reappeared, carrying a large parcel. He stopped at the wagon and said, "Y'all go down to that store and get the rest of it."

The rest of it, mostly food, included toys for children —the twenty-nine cent trinkets that in 1959 hung on racks in all Maine country stores—cans of cat food and a bag of grain for the chickens. By the time Hawkeye, Trapper and Spearchucker had delivered this, Duke was in the restaurant where, at 11:30 on a sunny spring morning, Laurier Castonguay was well in the bag.

The surgeons, having delivered their share of the largesse and returned to the station wagon, heard noise from the restaurant and decided that Duke and Laurier Castonguay were in disagreement. They went to the restaurant, where their decision was confirmed. Duke, older and smaller than Laurier, hardly in fighting trim, was slowly but surely dragging his protesting quarry toward the door. Duke, somewhat short of breath, was in nowhere near the state of respiratory distress that afflicted Laurier Castonguay, whose resistance was diminishing and whose face was blue.

The surgeons came to Duke's assistance and picked up Laurier. "Whatcha want us to do with him?" asked Hawkeye.

"We're taking him with us," said Duke. "He can do the chores and show us where to fish. Maybe we can beat some smarts into this dumb swamp canary."

"What is a swamp canary?" asked Spearchucker.

"A frog," replied Trapper John.

Duke, with Laurier subdued in the station wagon, revisited Amiko and explained that they'd hired her husband as a guide for their fishing trip and asked, "Does he get out of breath easy?"

"Oh yes, Doctor Duke. That's why he no work in woods and cut the pulp, him. He got no wind, him."

"In Maine," said Duke, "they think I talk funny, but

118

that Japanese Canuck of yours is real different."

"What?" asked Amiko.

"You pack up, Amiko. You and the kids and Laurier are moving out of here in a few days."

Amiko's pride was working, but pride can work just so hard. All of a sudden the phenomenon recurred. Amiko gave Duke an ear-to-ear grin.

With Laurier half-drunk and gasping for breath in the back of the wagon, the surgeons resumed their journey to Lake Chesuncook. "What are you going to do with your guest?" Hawkeye asked Duke.

"Wait'll he sobers up. If he behaves himself he can guide for us and do the chores. If he doesn't, I'll drown the bastard."

In Moose Bend the public reaction to Laurier's abduction fell far short of consternation, but someone casually mentioned it to Jack Marvin, the state cop from Greenville. Jack was making his weekly tour of Moose Bend in search of stolen cars. His interview with Amiko confused him, but he was forced to conclude that Laurier had been spirited away against his will and that a crime had been committed. Amiko innocently identified Dr. Duke as one of the kidnappers.

By the time the surgeons reached Doggy Moore's island, Laurier Castonguay, having achieved relative sobriety, was demanding to know what was going on. "You're working for us. You are our guide," explained Duke.

"I ain't gon work for you, you, you son beech."

"Now, look here, Laurier," said Spearchucker, "how about working for me?"

Laurier inspected Dr. Jones, assessed his attitude and decided that mature judgment called for quiet acquiescence. "Okay, you. I work for you, me," he agreed.

There was time for a few hours of fishing. Laurier did have talent as a guide, and they returned with six big salmon for supper. Waiting at the island were Jack Marvin and two game wardens he'd recruited as deputies.

"Evening, gentlemen," Hawkeye greeted the law. "Surely you cannot be in search of wrongdoers in this unspoiled natural paradise."

"You men are suspected of kidnapping. Laurier, did you come here willingly?"

"No, by Jeez."

"Which of you is Dr. Forrest?" asked the State Trooper.

"I am," said Duke.

"He's the one who done it," said Hawkeye. "Us three other guys is innocent, us. Ain't we, Laurier?"

"No, by Jeez."

"Okay, gentlemen, may I have your names?" requested Trooper Marvin.

"Sure," said Hawkeye. "Me, I'm Jean Beliveau."

"Maurice Richard," Said Trapper John.

"Happy to make your acquaintance, officer," said Spearchucker. "My name's Bernard Geoffrion, but my admirers call me Boom-Boom."

Trooper Marvin wrote down their names and told them to get their things together and accompany him to Greenville, where he would lock them up.

"Guess again," said Duke. "We're not coming. Why don't you just take Laurier home and ask Amiko who she'd rather have locked up. Me or her husband?"

"I'm afraid I can't do it that way," the trooper informed him.

"So shoot us," suggested Jean Beliveau.

"Go on, officer," urged Boom-Boom Geoffrion. "Shoot us. You fellers, too," he said, including the wardens in the invitation. "Start shooting."

Trooper Marvin for five years had been the only state cop in a vast area of northern Maine because he was one of the few on the force capable of handling the job. The average state cop would have become confused at this point, but Jack Marvin began to get a message.

"Well," he said, "I guess you gentlemen aren't going to come peacefully and I'm not justified in shooting you. The fact is, if I shoot anybody today, I'd like to shoot Laurier Castonguay. I've been thinking about it for five years."

"Good thinking," said Jean Beliveau.

"How about staying for supper?" asked Rocket Richard.

"You're very kind," said Trooper Marvin. "Laurier," he ordered, "get to work. I'd like to see you work."

"By Jeez, I feex you," growled Laurier.

"Now Laurier," counseled Boom-Boom Geoffrion, "don't be unpleasant. Clean the fish, build a fire, and I'll prepare drinks for everyone but you."

As the group relaxed and sipped Scotch whiskey around the fire Laurier built in Doggy Moore's big field-stone fireplace, Trooper Marvin seemed for a while lost in thought. Unlike the two wardens, who were just confused by it all, Jack Marvin knew that something unusual was going on. He didn't want to blow it. He knew, particularly, that Amiko Castonguay had a hard life, and if these screwballs wanted to help her, he was all for it.

Finally he asked Duke, "Doctor, will you tell me what you are up to?"

"Sure," said Duke. "Ah'm gonna put Laurier in the

121

hospital and find out why he can't breathe well, and ah'm gonna move Amiko and the kids to Crabapple Cove and put them up in a house I know of there. Then, when Laurier gets out of the hospital, he's either going to work and take care of his family, or I'll get him put away somewhere."

"What house do you have in mind?" asked Jean Beliveau, the former Hawkeye Pierce.

"Your old house."

"That's what I figured."

"Boom-Boom," Trooper Marvin said, "you guys will have to go through Greenville on your way home. Is there any chance you and Mr. Richard and Mr. Beliveau could stop by at my house on your way through?"

"Sure, glad to. Why?"

"Well," explained Trooper Marvin, "I have three teenage boys and they're all crazy about hockey."

"We're leaving here Tuesday," said Boom-Boom. "We'd be delighted to stop by and meet the kids."

Trooper Marvin thought his request might disconcert Boom-Boom Geoffrion. When it didn't, Trooper Marvin began to laugh.

"What's funny?" asked Boom-Boom.

"Dr. Jones, I just made you. The word in my organization is that any trooper has a head injury, we get Dr. Jones."

"Can I still say hello to your kids?" asked Spearchucker.

"My kids would probably rather meet Spearchucker Jones than even Boom-Boom Geoffrion."

"They'll want to meet me, too," said Rocket Richard. "I'm the real McCoy."

"Officer," ordered a slightly mulled Jean Beliveau,

"Arrest that man. He's an impostor."

"I'm not arresting anybody, but I'm likely to have you all committed. What about Laurier? You want to keep him?"

"Why don't you take him with you and get him down to the Spruce Harbor General. I'll send orders with you. By the time we get back we'll have some information."

"I ain't gon no hospital," protested Laurier.

"Jail, then?" asked Trooper Marvin.

"I no do nothin'."

"That's the charge, Laurier."

"Son beech."

When the fishermen passed through Greenville a few days later they stopped at Jack Marvin's, where 78 percent of the town's children had gathered to meet Spearchucker Jones. Fifty-seven percent of those present had never heard of either Boom-Boom Geoffrion or Spearchucker and would have accepted him as either, but the others were sufficiently impressed. Dr. Jones walked among his admirers, shook hands and had a word with everyone while Rocket Richard, Jean Beliveau and Duke Forrest sat in the station wagon drinking beer.

"I wish I was famous, too," Duke complained.

"So be famous," suggested Jean Beliveau. "Go out there and steal his thunder."

"Who'll I be?"

"Tough call," said the Rocket. "They never heard of anybody."

Jean Beliveau got out of the car and spoke to a small group of mid-teenagers. "Hey, you guys wanta meet Mickey Mantle? That's him, there, in the back of the station wagon."

In 1959, even in Greenville, Maine, Mickey Mantle

had been heard of. Within minutes the wagon was surrounded and Dr. Jones was left with only Jack Marvin to talk to.

"Your trade seems to have fallen off," Rocket Richard said to Spearchucker.

"What's going on?" asked Trooper Marvin.

"Who cares about nigger fullbacks when you can meet Mickey Mantle?" asked Jean Beliveau.

"Oh, my God," moaned the state policeman. "Dr. Jones, I really appreciate your coming, but I think you and Mr. Richard and Mr. Beliveau and Mr. Mantle had better get a move on. I see our local newspaper photographer and he's bound to want pictures. I'm sure Mr. Mantle doesn't want his picture in the *Bangor Daily News.*"

As the station wagon with Hawkeye Pierce (the former Jean Beliveau) at the wheel sped out of Greenville, Duke Forrest was needling his companion in the back seat. "You a real uppity nigra, Jones. I guess I showed you some White Power."

"Oh, that's okay, Duke. You guys just proved what so many of my brothers claim is true, but even I haven't believed it until now."

"What's that?"

"The black race is superior."

"How do you figure that?"

"The question does not deserve an answer."

As the week progressed, information on Laurier Castonguay accumulated while Amiko and her children were moved into their new home—Hawkeye's old house on the brink of Crabapple Cove. The radiologist reported that Laurier's left lung was hyperaerated, which means, simply, there was too much air in it, which suggested that air was trapped in it—that air could get in easier than it could get out. Hawkeye looked in with his bronchoscope and discovered that the main bronchial tube that carries air to the left lung was narrowed down to a pinpoint. This explained Laurier's shortness of breath.

Duke, like most veterans of Mobile Army Surgical Hospitals in Korea, had brought records of all his cases home with him. In his old records he discovered that he had taken care of L. Castonguay at the 4077th MASH. Given that information, it was easy to decide that the bullet which traversed Laurier's chest had caused injury resulting in nearly complete occlusion of the left main bronchus.

Duke and Hawkeye performed surgery that eliminated the bronchial stricture. Jocko Allcock, armed with facts supplied by the surgeons and his natural touch with Veterans Affairs, rapidly established that, for seven years, Laurier Castonguay should have been receiving 100 percent disability pay from the Veterans Administration. He presented Amiko with a check for $30,000 the day Laurier was discharged from the hospital.

While in the hospital various nonsurgical tests revealed a previously unsuspected fact. Laurier Castonguay was not stupid. He'd just never been exposed to anything. During his recovery period Laurier and Amiko were tutored in basic reading, writing and arithmetic by Mrs. Pierce, Mrs. Jones and Mrs. Forrest. Amiko Castonguay was the proudest and happiest person in the world, a few months later, when she was accepted for a six-month surgical technician's course at the new Spruce Harbor Medical Center. For Amiko to be working at the operating table with Dr. Duke, the Greatest Man in the

World, was an impossible dream come true.

Laurier, breathing normally, learning to be a part of the world, quit the booze and became the man of the family. Dr. Pierce prevailed upon his uncle, Lew the Jew Pierce, to take on Laurier as an apprentice in the lobster-catching profession. Lew, recalcitrant at first, declared that he wouldn't have "no lily pad jumper hauling lobsters in Muscongus Bay." When Hawkeye offered to spring for one hundred new traps and suggested that Laurier do 80 percent of the work for 40 percent of the money, Lew meditated deeply.

"Come on, Jew," urged his nephew. "How can you lose? You'll have more income and less work. Your golf game has to improve. Whadda yuh say?"

"I'll give it a try," said Lew.

With Amiko and Laurier both making a living, everything improved. Amiko, once she got the hang of it, turned out to be a good student. By 1962 she had passed a high school equivalency test and been accepted at the nursing school down in Portland.

As I said in the beginning, I get a certain amount of heat about Duke Forrest being sort of a teacher's pet, but that's the only beef I've had in the ten years that Amiko Castonguay, R.N., has been my Operating Room Supervisor.

8
PSYCHOANALYSIS

BEGINNING a week or so before Thanksgiving and continuing into early January, surgery at Spruce Harbor Medical Center slows down. Folks don't want to have elective procedures done during the holidays, and the surgical staff likes to start skiing or just take it easy.

As administrator, I approach this season with apprehension because when my surgeons are not totally consumed by surgical responsibility they tend to get me in trouble. I got my first sniff of trouble about a week before Thanksgiving 1974 in the coffee shop when I overheard a conversation between Pierce, Forrest, Jones, McIntyre and Solly (Wolfman) Davis, the bearded Afro-haired psychiatrist. Wolfman was saying, "Rex Eatapuss will be back from his course in advanced Freudian psychoanalysis, or whatever·these phonies call it, on December 1. I think you guys should undergo analysis."

"Not me," said Trapper John. "I'm okay. I'm TM'ing it."

"What's that mean?" Duke asked.

"Transcendental masturbation. I sit in a corner, but I don't say my mantra. I just contemplate my equipment."

"It come natural or you have to take lessons?" Hawkeye asked.

"I'm self-taught. Cheaper than paying a hundred

127

bucks for that course in Meditation they're giving down at Androscoggin College."

"You capable of total contemplation?"

"Not quite. Spearchucker's the one who oughta go into analysis. I was reading about him in *Sports Illustrated* the other day. They said when he was with the Eagles he was a big, mean, aggressive, hostile nigger. You realize we got something like that right in our midst?"

"I could fix him," Wolfman volunteered. "Give him a little Central Maine Power. Turn him into a sissy."

Spearchucker just grinned his slow ear-to-ear, white-of-eye-popping grin.

"Don't grin too long, Chucker," Duke pleaded. "I can't stand the glare. You know I heard a rumor. I heard Hooker and Rex Eatapuss made some kind of deal—got some federal money for a psychoanalysis program in that damnfool Mental Health Center. I hear they don't get the money unless the medical staff undergoes analysis."

"I'll believe anything," said Hawkeye. "The wolf lobby is on Jerry Ford cuz he gave Brezhnev a wolfskin coat. Christly wolves got more power down there than the AMA."

"Shoulda given the bastard a live wolf coat," Duke suggested.

"I don't think the Hook thinks we'll hold still for Rex Eatapuss psychoanalyzing us," from Spearchucker.

"Oh, hell," said Trapper. "You know how those things work. The government's so crazy you gotta go along with a few things to get the money you need. Let's enjoy it."

This brilliant conversation was interrupted by the page system ordering Doctors Pierce and McIntyre to

128

surgery. I was relieved that for the moment there wouldn't be open rebellion. The Mental Health Clinic is an integral part of our overall health-care effort, and I did get a hundred grand just by agreeing to have my staff psychoanalyzed.

Late that same afternoon Dr. Pierce stopped in for a touch of Scotch from my office jug. He looked tired. "Jesus," he groaned after a sip of Chivas Regal, "I'm sure used up. Got up at four o'clock this morning for a GI bleeder, spent the whole morning in the O.R. and four solid hours in that office."

"That's more office time than usual for you, isn't it?" I asked.

"Yeah. Ever since Mrs. Ford and Happy Rockefeller had their trouble, the broads have gone bananas feeling their breasts. Then they have their doctors feel their breasts. The doctors are all so eager not to miss anything they feel lumps that ain't there and refer them to surgeons. Christ, half the time you take them broads in and do a biopsy just to make everybody happy. Know goddamn well nothing wrong."

"There've been a few cases turn up, haven't there, as a result of all the publicity?"

"Yeah, there have, so I don't complain too much. Just had one that's gonna be bad news. Broad named Rankin. Her husband's the Pope of the Supreme Spirit Church, or whatever. He's the head Supreme Spirit of the whole state. Mealymouthed, nasty pious, dumb bastard. Wife's a little broad, maybe forty, couple kids. I knew she was terrified the minute she came in. Christ, Doggy'd examined her just ten days ago, said she was okay, but she'd found something in her right breast, and she was right. I figure even money it's malignant, so I tell the Pope to come in, give 'em both the routine: if it's malignant, the breast goes. Mrs. Rankin was really shook. This jerk husband gave me the "we've committed our bodies and souls to Jesus Christ, His will be done" routine. I didn't know these gomers really talked that way. I despise him, and I only spent fifteen minutes with him. He was telling me he knows all about I'm a fine surgeon, I am the right hand of God gonna cut his wife's right breast. I hope the thing's benign. If it's malignant and a year from now she has a recurrence, I can see this Jesus freak praying over the poor woman. Christ, you could tell she's his chattel, not his wife. What she'll want and need is him to put his arm around her and say, 'Honey, I love you, we'll fight it all the way.' He is just a cold-blooded, Bible-spewing grunt."

When Hawkeye was on his second drink, my phone rang. The caller was the Reverend Mr. Rankin, Pope of the Church of the Supreme Spirit. He explained about his wife, told me about arrangements for her surgery by Dr. Pierce. He was, however, in a terrible dither because, as he left Dr. Pierce's office, he had seen a glassful of an obviously alcoholic beverage sitting atop the refrigerator in the little kitchenette one passes on the way out.

"No one, I repeat, no one," the Reverend repeated, "who uses alcohol will touch my beloved wife. I want your advice as to whom else I may employ to perform the delicate work required, someone whose lips have never touched the devil's brew."

"May I call you back?" I asked.

"Of course, Mr. Hooker. We place ourselves in your hands."

Addressing my Chief of Surgery, I asked, "You been belting the devil's brew in your office?"

"Huh?"

"That was the Reverend Mr. Rankin. He wants a different surgeon. He says you had a drink on top of your refrigerator."

"For chrissake, that's iced tea. Half of Spruce Harbor knows I drink iced tea in the office! You know it!"

"Yeah," I said, "I know it, but I thought maybe you'd like to get off the hook. If, as you think, this is a trouble case, you're bound to tangle with the Reverend sooner or later. Maybe it'll save trouble if we get Duke to take the case. He's not quite as opinionated, prejudiced and anti-Christ as you are."

"Duke, of course, doesn't drink. You think maybe that stuff he has shipped up from Georgia is pure spring water? Christ, his family's been cookin' shine since the dawn of time."

I pointed out, "If we try to find a surgeon who doesn't drink, we'll have to ship the lady to Africa and have her hunt up a missionary. It'll have to be Duke."

"That's okay," Hawk agreed. "In fact, as you suggest, it's a great relief, but I don't like the idea of that klutz spreading it around that I drink during office hours."

"Maybe you should start," I suggested. "You're always complaining you got too much work. Why not drive a few of them off?" As soon as I said it, I was sorry.

"Hell, half my patients would want to join me. Since I've been back here, I've operated on two hundred people I've been drinking with, here or there, one time or another."

"Yeah, I guess that's right. Will you call Duke and explain? Then I'll call the Reverend and complete the arrangements."

"Sure," agreed Dr. Pierce. "Finestkind."

Surgery was scheduled for three days later. In the interim I worried, hoped and prayed (well, almost) that all would be well with Mrs. Rankin. Also, I endured a barrage of comments from my staff about their forthcoming psychoanalysis.

Attitudes diverged. Boom-Boom Benner was openly enthusiastic, begged Rex Eatapuss to take him first. Rex Eatapuss, for whatever reason, did not, at least outwardly, respond with comparable enthusiasm. Duke, always the most sensitive, concerned, involved, told Rex over coffee, "Ah sure hope yuh all can cure Trapper from contemplatin'. "

And on and on. Duke operated on Mrs. Rankin one Friday morning. Although Hawkeye and Duke had both thought the lump in her breast was malignant, it turned out to be a benign harmless cyst.

That evening Graveyard Alice, out of Bette Bang Bang's stable, attended services at the Spirit Church, accompanied by Jocko Allcock, whom she introduced to Reverend Rankin as her husband. The loving couple expressed a strong desire for salvation, explaining that, singly and together, they had indulged in more sin than your average everyday churchgoer. The Reverend Mr. Rankin, assessing Alice, correctly decided that her case merited special, intense, individual effort, and suggested an hour of prayer on Saturday afternoon. This worked out nicely because Mrs. Rankin was still in the hospital and Alice didn't work until 9 P.M.

To save Alice, the Reverend Mr. Rankin visited her in the semiplush apartment she sometimes shares with Jocko Allcock.

The Saturday afternoon group in the Bay View included most of my surgical staff and others prominent in

132

the community. The weather was poor, skiing negligible, the deer season over, no golf, nothing to do, and all were there, waiting for news of Alice's salvation. Finally at 3:28 Jocko arrived with the word. "He done saved her in fifteen minutes. Spent the next hour exercising her. Alice says he won't touch no booze, but come to exercise he ain't exactly what you'd call abstemious."

"Male and female, them Spirits always been strong horizontal," volunteered the historian, Lew the Jew. "But, Jesus, boy, I tell you, they can't cook worth a goddamn. Want to go to a good church supper, go to the Rollers. Course, afterwards, to the Rollers, even if a feller gets him a piece, tain't no good. Depends, I s'pose, on what a feller likes."

"Well," thought Trapper, "as long as we have both right here in our fair city, there's really no problem. We have the best of both worlds."

"I've decided to become a lush," Hawkeye Pierce announced, apropos of nothing and out of a clear sky. Possibly because he'd been considered a semilush for twenty years, this statement caused not even a riffle of conversational reaction.

"I said," he repeated petulantly, "I'm gonna become a lush."

"Another martini—make it a double—for the lush," Trapper ordered, then asked, "What is your mission?"

"I wish to decrease the size of my surgical practice. Also I think I will go foolish and get Rex Eatapuss to lay a cure on me, employing the technique of Sigmund Freud."

"Tight end, Kansas City Chiefs," chimed in Schweinhund Wincapaw, one of Crazy Horse Weinstein's champion peddlers of fine gents' apparel.

133

The group mulled this statement momentarily before its spokesman, Jocko Allcock, asked, "Whadda you talkin' about, Schweinhund?"

"Six four, two twenty, Alcorn A&M, Kansas City Chiefs," Schweinhund recited proudly.

"May I paraphrase Mr. Allcock's question, Schweinhund?" asked Trapper. "To what or whom do you refer?"

"Sigmund Freud."

Spearchucker was able to clear up the misunderstanding. "You're thinking of Julius Freud, Schweinhund. He's the guy with the Chiefs. Sigmund Freud was a honkie headshrinker who promulgated the Freudian theory which is: Everything wrong with you is because you are pissed off at either your father or your mother."

"I love my parents," said Schweinhund.

"You're crazy, Schweinhund," said Hawkeye. "Anybody so uneducated he don't know enough to hate one of his parents gotta have help. What you need is Mental Health. I'll arrange an appointment for you with Rex Eatapuss, who has just finished an advanced course in modern Freudian psychoanalysis."

"He'll get me all messed up," Schweinhund protested.

"That's the whole point," Hawkeye explained. "Look, Schweinhund, I've known you all my life. You're completely normal. Small drink, little smoke, hardly any strange stuff except when your wife visits her mother, pay your bills, own your own home, two kids in college getting good marks, vote the straight Republican ticket. Schweinhund, for chrissake, you don't even take tranquilizers. And I've seen you shoot 92 and smile. By any modern standards, you are a mental health disaster. Your problem is you're too dumb to know you're a disaster. Rex Eatapuss will explain to you why you are a disaster, which will make you nervous. Then you can go to Wolfman who will help you by giving you Valium or Lithium or electricity and get you into the mainstream of society. You know, Schwein, I bet you're such a square you like H. R. Haldeman better than Ralph Ellsberg."

"You are one crazy sonovabitch, Pierce," said Schweinhund.

"You are right. Spread the word, will you, I've flipped. Get it all over town. I'm gonna have one more mart and then I gotta go buy a book for that stemmy Christer."

"What book are you going to buy him?" asked Trapper.

"*The Joy of Sex.* What else? They got some great illustrations. Reverend Rankin will love it."

After buying *The Joy of Sex* and arranging for Halfaman Timberlake to substitute it for the Bible on the lectern at the Spirit Church, Dr. Pierce went home, watched a football game on TV and went to bed early. At midnight, down in Tedium Cove, two Simmons boys, which ones don't matter, had a shotgun shootout. Both were shot in the chest. Although not on call, Hawkeye was the only chest surgeon who could be found. By 8 A.M. he had removed half a lung from each Simmons.

When I went to the hospital about nine o'clock Sunday morning, just to look around, I found Pierce and an exhausted O.R. crew drinking coffee. Pierce was even smoking a cigarette, which he hardly ever does anymore. He looked asleep even as he sipped coffee.

"Good morning, hard working administrator type," he greeted me. "I trust you are rested, refreshed, that you

135

are restored, replenished. Surely, this being the case, you will take me to the Bay View for some morning sustenance."

"Certainly, if you say so. You going to change your clothes first?"

At the Bay View Dr. Pierce ordered veal scallopini, scrambled eggs, spaghetti with clam sauce and a double bloody Mary. Halfway through this snack he said, "Look, Hook, I am physically and emotionally exhausted. There's just too much work. I'm almost fifty years old and instead of reaching some nice, easy plateau, I'm working harder than when I was an intern. And I don't seem to know how to get off the treadmill. We keep bringing in new people and I try to fence off the work, but look at last night. What the hell. Trapper and Boom-Boom won't take calls for anything but cardiovascular stuff. I don't blame them, but that leaves me with every chest emergency whether I'm on call or not. Try to get another chest guy in, he doesn't want to take care of gunshot wounds, he wants to do aortocoronary bypasses. That leaves me the grunt who takes care of the grunts who shoot each other or hit trees with their cars and break their ribs and puncture their lungs. And, baby, I'm about used up. I have reached the point where I don't want to talk to anyone, see anyone. I just want to be left alone."

"Well," I said, "why don't you pack it in and leave for a month. Not even you are indispensable. The world would go on."

"I would, but I got a solid schedule for two weeks. I think I'll plan a month off after that. Meanwhile I think I'll try to tarnish my image. Also, I'm going to bring my old secretary, Lucinda McIntyre, out of retirement to

136

work for me in the hospital. Maybe if she'll do the talking I can keep up with the work. But now I'm going home and go to bed and take the phones off the hook. See you tomorrow."

That night there was snow, a foot of it. I got in a little late Monday morning. Already the hospital was buzzing. It seems that Dr. Pierce was making rounds in tennis shorts, sneakers and a T-shirt with the legend "Finest-kind Clinic and Fish Market." He was followed by Mrs. McIntyre, who carried a notepad, a stethoscope and a bottle of Seagrams 7. As he visited each patient, he'd have a pop from the bottle and exclaim, "Day like this, fella needs a little pop, get him goin', get ready to go in there and do that surgery."

By nine o'clock the idiot was doing a pneumonectomy on Danny Cotton of Deer Isle, and I summoned Mrs. McIntyre to my office.

"Explain!" I commanded.

"What?"

"You know what."

"If Dr. Pierce wants to be ready for tennis, what business is it of yours?"

"How about the booze?"

"It's iced tea."

"Yeah, but——"

"Dr. Pierce said it was your idea."

I groaned and told her to get lost.

Hawkeye followed the pneumonectomy with the repair of a hiatus hernia that Benny Scrubbs, the pro from Wawenock, claimed was screwing up his putting because every time he bent over he burped. After that it was one o'clock and there were two feet of snow. Not much was moving. Office hours were canceled. Dr.

Pierce, in his tennis costume, reinforced by an ankle-length bearskin coat inherited from his grandfather, accompanied by Lucinda, mounted his jeep pickup with attached snowplow and plowed his way to the Bay View for lunch.

Only Angelo and a few semistranded doctors were present. They couldn't get home, and hanging in the Bay View was more fun than the hospital. Lucinda situated her employer in a corner, gave him a martini, *The New York Times* and the *Boston Globe,* and placed on a table in front of him an artistically designed and lettered proclamation, a product of her own artistry but conceived by Dr. Pierce. It proclaimed:

I am not speaking to the following groups or individuals:
1) Psychoanalysts or people who go to them.
2) Psychologists.
3) Chiropractors.
4) Acupuncture flakes.
5) Vegetarians.
6) Orthodontists.
7) People who say "like" or "you know."
8) Gynecologists.
9) People who want moles or toenails removed.
10) People who talk about the weather.
11) The guy who put in the plumbing at HoJo's Motel in Portland because you can't reach the toilet paper without you got three arms.
12) Democrats.
13) Members of Rotary, Kiwanis, Lions, Elks, Masons, Knights of Columbus and Odd Fellows.
14) Any member of the Eastern Star, Good Luck Rebeccas, WCTU or DAR who is not young, good lucking and very horny.
15) Ministers, except rabbis and Episcopalians, some of whom ain't too bad.

16) Walter Cronkite, Dan Rather and Eric Clarified.
And 17, last, but by no means least, Dr. Albert Schwarzer,
the Spade Pediatrician.

As it turned out, the Bay View this day was about the only port in a storm. Snow, plus word of Pierce's activity, or lack of it, brought a sizable crowd. Inevitably, Mrs. McIntyre was bombarded with questions, for some of which she had previously prepared typed answers, with multiple copies. The first seven categories all received the same answer: "Dr. Pierce believes that this type person runs rabbits and barks at the moon."

When asked why Dr. Pierce was not speaking to gynecologists, the answer was: "Gynecologists can't see anybody who's sick for three months. They're too busy doing pelvic exams for $15. If your wife has something really wrong, the only guy who'll take care of her is a general surgeon, which is a good thing because if there's something really wrong you're better off with a general surgeon."

The answer on Democrats created some strong feeling, although, as Hawkeye pointed out to Angelo, the proprietor, not enough to cause a groundswell of measurable emotion because very few Democrats can afford to eat and drink in the Bay View. The answer was: "I ain't talking to Democrats because they are people who, if you don't give them everything they want, they'll steal it."

Hardly a customer escaped category number nine because fraternal organizations are very large in Spruce Harbor. The typed response to this and other categories was Hawkeye's common, oft used crypticism: "If I gotta explain, there's no use trying."

Timidly, tentatively, certain people approached Lucinda McIntyre to request an audience with the surgeon. Obviously, screening the applicants was simple, because no one qualified. Wooden Leg Wilcox came closest but was disqualified because, as he entered, he made reference to the persistence of the still falling snow, thereby establishing himself as a commentator on the weather.

A group of concerned friends gathered in another corner to discuss the situation and, with some logic, decided to call Solly Wolfman Reddy Kilowatt Davis in psychiatric consultation. Solly arrived and stamped snow all over the floor. After briefing, he asked Lucinda if it was permissible to submit questions in writing. She suggested that he do just that, but could not guarantee answers.

The first question submitted was: "Why are you wearing the tennis outfit?"

Soon he received a written reply: "Angelo says if I look good in the outfit, drink five marts and eat a pound of spaghetti, he can get me a tryout with the guinea Davis Cup team."

The questioning continued: "You did two major procedures this morning and here you are drinking. Suppose something goes wrong?"

Answer: "Trapper and Boom-Boom are covering me for the next month. I have canceled all other surgery and am going to plant palm trees on the hospital lawn."

Question: "What is your problem with Al Black?"

Answer: "Assuming that you refer to Dr. Albert Schwarzer, the Spade pediatrician who devotes his life to the care of underprivileged honkie kids, he stiffed me for a finn on a football bet. Surely you can understand my

140

righteous wrath, particularly since I hear you are a Puerto Rican."

Lucinda McIntyre, always sensitive to the rights and feelings of others, was forced to intercede by explaining to Hawkeye, "Dr. Pierce, my participation must terminate if you insist on further ethnic reference. Dr. Davis is Jewish."

"Looks more like an anarchist to me. Better check him for bombs. Now, I am going to start reading *Sports Illustrated*. I will tolerate no further interruptions. I will leave when you tell me the roads are passable. However, I will talk on the phone to Rod Laver, John Newcomb, Arthur Ashe and Chris Evert, if any of them should happen to call."

A voice in the background said, "The last time the stupid bastard flipped, he claimed Palmer and Nicklaus was paying him to stay off'n the tour."

A reporter, covering the event for the Spruce Harbor *Gazette*, asked Wolfman for a psychiatric evaluation of Dr. Pierce's performance. "In very simple, in fact in laymen's terms," said Wolfman, "he's not crazy. He's just a jerk."

Dr. Pierce, often more alert than he seems to be, overheard this. "Hey, you," he exhorted the minion of the press, "try for accuracy. You spell jerk with an *E*, not a *U*."

"I'm quite aware of that, Doctor."

"Ain't you the gomer does the sports on the radio?"

"Sometimes."

"Ain't you the gomer called the Vike quarterback Fran Tar Kenton? Ain't you the gomer who says Jew-Ann Marichal? Ain't you the gomer who called Wimbleton a prestidigious golf tournament?"

"We all make mistakes, Doctor."

"Yeah, but you never even learned to read, in addition to which you are a grunt, like everybody in the news business."

"Oh, lay off, Hawk," came a deep voice from an opposite corner, where Spearchucker Jones sat with Al Black, Duke and Boom-Boom Benner.

"Find out who said that," Hawkeye instructed Lucinda, "and put him on my black list."

"That does it, Hawkeye, I'm leaving. You fight your own silly battles."

"Just a minute before you leave, Lucinda," said Spearchucker. "Ask that honkie if he really wants another chest cutter around here, maybe a guy who could do vascular surgery and general surgery, too—young cat, hungry, got some smarts."

"Did you hear the question, Dr. Pierce?" Lucinda asked, sort of reluctantly.

"The answer is yes. Who is he, and when's he coming?"

"D'Artagnan Maguire, who has just finished his residency out in Iowa City, University of Iowa. With the Saints, briefly, backalong. Knee trouble. You must remember him. Played for Harvard."

"Oh. The Grambling of the North. You recommendin' him, Chucker? You know him?"

"I been talking to the chief out there. Kid could go anywhere. Talked to him about Spruce Harbor at meetings. Didn't know how much you were hurting. I got his number. Want me to call him?"

"Sure. Call him."

Fortunately, the call to Iowa City went through faster,

as is usual, than a call to Tedium Cove. Dr. Maguire had just left the O.R. Spearchucker brought the phone to Hawkeye, who said, "Hey, boy, I wanta take three months off and I got a lotta surgery lined up. You wanta come and do it? I'll make you a full partner, 50–50 right from the start."

Spearchucker hadn't even told Dr. Maguire who was calling. He and Lucinda listened in on Angelo's extension.

"Who is this?" asked D'Artagnan.

"Hawkeye Pierce. Spruce Harbor, Maine. Guarantee you at least forty G's a year take-home."

"Doctor, I know about Spruce Harbor, but I can't believe you're calling up a total stranger and making such an offer. What do you know about me?"

"The Chucker says you're okay."

"He doesn't really know me."

"Guy out there I talked to, Ken Griffin, does gastric bypasses, gimme the word on you. Don't worry. I know what I'm doing. Whadda yuh say? Yes or no?"

"Dr. Pierce, do you know that I'm black?"

"You're what?"

"Black."

"I can't believe that. Name like D'Artagnan Maguire, I figured you was a left-handed Nicaraguan ski jumper."

"The fact remains that I'm black. This conversation sounds a bit peculiar, sir."

"My professional corporation, which is called B. F. Pierce, MD-PA, will lay ten big ones on you if you show up for work a week from today. You are my first-round draft choice."

"I'd like to think about it."

"You one of them militant jigs?"

"Oh, man, now look here——"

"You can live in my house till you find a place. Me and Mary goin' to someplace warm, play some golf."

Spearchucker decided to intercede at this point. "Hey, boy, this is Jones. Don't look the gift hoss in the mouth. Pierce is crazy but he'll take good care of you. I say give it a try."

"Hey, D'Artagnan," Pierce interrupted, "I know this is a touch sudden, but I been looking and a lotta guys don't want to come here, or their wives don't, but you can do lots of surgery and if your social conscience is bothering you, let me assure you we got lots of underprivileged for you to take care of, unless you're prejudiced against white underprivileged."

"Well——"

"By the way," Hawkeye interrupted, "you got house apes?"

"What?"

"House apes, for chrissake. You got kids?"

"I have two children, ages six and three."

"Finestkind. You move into Mansion Pierce till I get back, take care of my house apes, ages ten, ten, thirteen and fifteen. They'll take care of your house apes nights you want to go out. Come to think of it, you go for that deal, you really are a dumb nigger."

"I'll be there, Doctor. I gotta find out what makes you tick."

"Finestkind. Hey, boy, whadda I call yuh? I mean, like, you know, man, like, you know I can't stand at the operating table, like, you know, and say, like, 'Clamp that bleeder, D'Artagnan.' Incidentally, if you say 'like' and 'you know' the deal's off."

"Call me Frenchy, and I don't talk that way."

144

"Holy Mother of Jesus," groaned Hawkeye. "Get here as fast as you can, Frenchy."

The snow had stopped. Dr. Pierce decided that he wanted to demonstrate his serve, which he'd been practicing at the new indoor courts. The first serve knocked two drinks off the table where Spearchucker was sitting with his friends.

"We'll go now, Hawkeye," Lucinda said.

"Where we goin'?"

"I'm afraid that, under the circumstances, you'll have to stay with the McIntyres."

"Hot dog. You gonna show me where the bum hid the money?"

"I'll break your skull, that's what I'll do," Lucinda promised. "Now put on that foolish coat and let's get out of here."

There's usually some drift ice in the channel between the McIntyre's home on Thief Island and the dock at the Finestkind Clinic and Fish Market, although it seldom freezes solid. Hawkeye bade Lucinda navigate while he stood in the bow, bearskin coat over tennis costume, brandishing tennis racket and yelling, "Row, you bastards, we gotta catch them jeezly Redcoats."

Lucinda told me the next day that, after his reenactment of Washington crossing the Delaware, the great surgeon subsided somewhat and changed into some of Trapper's old clothes. He mixed another drink, helped build a big fire in the fireplace, turned on Merv Griffin and said, "Okay, I'm going to drink myself to sleep by nine o'clock but first I want a big steak and a big salad. In the morning I am going back to work until this new kid gets in from Iowa City."

Lucinda said, "I'm sure he's competent, but what

makes you think your patients will hold still for him suddenly taking over?"

"You'll be surprised. A few will rebel, but most of them will take my word that he's okay. It's a funny thing about prejudice around here. When I was first in practice, there was more prejudice against me because I'm a Pierce from Crabapple Cove than there will be against Frenchy Maguire. That's partly because Chucker, Dr. Albert Schwarzer, the other guys have broken the ice, but it's also a definite phenomenon of rural Maine. Not to say there isn't prejudice. The middle class, the shopkeepers, the gomers we send to the legislature, that kind, are the biggest problem. I was up in Augusta having breakfast at the Senator Motel early one morning backalong. Heard some legislative gomers cussing out Ben Brown, the black guy we got running the State energy program. You'da thought, for chrissake, it was the Ku Klux Klan."

"Isn't this group most of your practice?"

"True, but they're easily cowed. They don't like it, the hell with 'em."

"Really," Lucinda asked, "why a black, anyhow? It's not as though we had a black population."

"It's not that he's black. It's just that he has the right kind of training for this particular job. Trapper and Boom-Boom can use him, too. White guys coming out of the big leagues look down their noses at us, as their wives do. Christ, I've had a couple honkies down, made them the same offer, taken 'em in the Bay View, somebody calls a guy a nigger, they figure we're a bunch of barbarians. The same cats find out the jigs belong to the country club, you can see that buggin' 'em, too. Funny world. Incidentally, I already knew about this guy. I've checked

146

him out six ways from Jesus. He'll be okay."

The next morning, a Tuesday, Pierce and Lucinda appeared again, early, on rounds. This time the great surgeon was dressed normally in scrub suit and white coat. Lucinda carried a sheaf of papers, one of which she handed to everyone who came near them. It said:

1. Yes, it sure was one helluva storm.
2. No, I didn't have any trouble getting in this morning.
3. Yes, with this wind, it sure does tend to drift.
4. Yes, it's cold enough for me. Gonna turn colder tonight, I heard on the news.
5. Yes, they called off school over my way. The plows haven't gotten around to all the side roads.
6. I don't know how cold it was at my house this morning, and you wouldn't be asking if you weren't sure it was colder at your house than my house so buzz off and let me go about my business, or I'll have somebody break your kneecaps.

Arriving at the Intensive Care Unit, Dr. Pierce discovered that a chest drainage tube had been clamped off while the patient went for a walk. Since the patient had a constant air leak following a lobectomy, and since he had specifically ordered that the tube not be clamped, he was on the verge of a temper tantrum.

"Now, now, Doctor," said Lucinda, "please let me take care of it. Remember, you aren't talking today." She hurried him out of the unit, backed him into a corner. "I know your routine. It does no good to rant and rave about the hospital being a home for retarded females and so forth ad nauseam. I already know about this. There was a new nurse on last night, and she misunderstood. She's terribly upset, and I want you to break your

147

silence and explain to her nicely why the tube shouldn't have been clamped and to assure her that no real harm was done."

"Which one? That big redhead?" asked Hawkeye. "Maybe I'll ask her if she'd like to shack up. In fact, that's exactly what I'll do. Let's go."

"Oh, no, you don't. There'll be none of that."

"Okay, Lucinda. Then you tell that dumb wool when I say a chest tube isn't to be clamped, it's because clamping it could get the patient in serious trouble. And if she ever does it again I'll run her out of town. Furthermore——"

"Oh, shut up, Hawkeye. Not another word, particularly of the kind you're so fond of."

"Ain't my fault I grew up a grunt."

"Oh, just please shut up."

Well, that's how it went the rest of the week. Hawkeye communicated through Lucinda, did his surgery and postponed everything that could be postponed in the office.

Dr. and Mrs. D'Artagnan Maguire arrived from Iowa City on Friday afternoon and moved directly into the Pierce home in Crabapple Cove. When Hawkeye got home from work, he found his twins, Jim and Ann, showing their guests how to drive a snowmobile.

Hawkeye met the Maguires in the kitchen. I gather that the guests felt a trifle awkward until Big Benjy Pierce, Hawkeye's still-robust father, dropped in with some lobsters for supper. Big Benjy'd been out hauling traps most of the fairly cold day and had worked through the best part of a pint of Old Bantam Whiskey. His arrival tended to break the ice. Benjy has a collection of stories, all untrue, which he uses on outsiders. After half

148

an hour Frenchy Maguire and his pretty wife were well broken up with laughter. From then on, Hawk says, it was easy. Frenchy adjusted easily to being called "Boy" when he figured out that Benjy calls everybody "Boy."

Hawkeye and Frenchy came to see me in my office after rounds on Saturday morning. With some embarrassment I brought up the bit about the staff being psychoanalyzed. To my relief, neither surgeon seemed a bit upset. They even suggested a Tuesday appointment with Rex Eatapuss. I should have known.

By Tuesday, Frenchy had met all of Hawkeye's inpatients and several of the future surgical patients. In the O.R. Monday morning he did a pneumonectomy and a gallbladder, assisted by Hawkeye. Any doubts about Frenchy's ability and personality had been dispelled by four o'clock Tuesday afternoon when, rigged with a recording device by Trapper John, someone went to be psychoanalyzed by Dr. Rex Eatapuss.

As I said, I should have known. The someone was not Frenchy Maguire. God save us, it was the curator of the Port Waldo town dump, one Juicy (Big Dumpsmell) Larkin. As I pieced it together later, Frenchy, hearing about Rex Eatapuss, stated firmly that, rather than submit to such an indignity, he would return to Iowa City.

Hawkeye told me afterwards, "I wasn't too upset when Frenchy said no to that foolishness. If we get to the point where a high-class cat like Frenchy can't work until he's psychoanalyzed by a moron like Rex, then I'm cutting for Canada. What's more, none of my gang is going to hold still for it either. You can take that hundred grand and stick it in some Democrat's ear."

"Okay, okay," I agreed. "I'll get around it, somehow. But for chrissake, how and why Juicy Larkin?"

"Well, Rex has never seen Frenchy, and he's so dumb he wouldn't know a nigger from a giraffe. My brain trust and I decided that Juicy would be a good substitute. He'd try a goat with the mumps for twenty bucks and a case of beer, so there was no problem in enlisting his services."

I still marveled that even a group as eccentric as Hawkeye Pierce and his brain trust would select Juicy. For one thing, he is not black, although, come to think of it, he does look a lot like one of the old black-face vaudevillians. Dirt and soot from his fires on the dump coat not only his face but all of him. Unshaven, slovenly, forty-six years old, about five eleven and 240 pounds. Juicy has to be one of our less prepossessing citizens. I don't know whether, as Hawkeye alleges, he likes goats, but somehow he has bestowed fourteen children upon the community. And I do mean on the community. Food stamps will never go begging.

At my behest, Hawkeye described the recruiting of Juicy Larkin. He and Wooden Leg went out to the dump on a Sunday. The interview went about like this.

Hawkeye: "Hi, Juicy. How they goin'?"

Juicy: "Finestkind."

Hawkeye: "You wanna make twenty bucks and a case of beer, Juicy?"

Juicy: "Ayuh. What I gotta do?"

Hawkeye: "Get psychoanalyzed by Rex Eatapuss."

Juicy: "By the Jesus."

Hawkeye: "Well, whadda yuh say, Juice. Give it a try?"

Juicy: "Jesus, boy. I dunno. That Rex, ain't he quee-ah? I don't want him messin' around."

Hawkeye: "He won't mess around. All you gotta do is

be on a couch and talk to him. Just your normal conversation will be okay."

Juicy: "I gotta problem. Been savin' my money, take a crack at Graveyard Alice, but I keep havin' financial difficulties."

Hawkeye: "You do drive a hard bargain, Juicy. But okay. You go into Bette Bang Bang's and me and Wooden Leg'll see you're taken care of."

Juicy: "My pickup's done broken down. You'll have to take me in your own self."

Wooden Leg: "Tain't no problem. Jump right into Hawk's Mercedes. Get in back, Juicy. Make yourself comfortable."

As they drove toward Spruce Harbor, Hawkeye was somewhat piqued. "I'll never get this car deodorized," he complained to Leg. "Smell's like we got the whole Steeler defense before they showered plus about six goats in here."

At Bette Bang Bang's they knocked on the door and waited while Bette inspected them to make sure they were legitimate customers. Juicy's lips moistened, he slobbered just a touch and his eyes were beginning to pop outwards.

Whenever someone like Hawkeye and Wooden Leg appeared, Bette was suspicious, but, reluctantly, she let the three of them in.

"Whadda yuh want?" she asked in her dulcet voice.

"We wanta fix Juicy up with Alice. We're payin', me and Leg."

"Cost double and he's gotta have a bath first and burn his clothes. I got some old clothes lyin' around he can have. Ain't fancy, but they're clean. Alice won't be back for an hour nohow. She's gitten' saved by the Reverend Rankin."

"Maybe you better make him the house chaplain," suggested Leg.

"Like to give the horny sonovabitch the next dose of clap we get around here," Bette growled. "He don't pay nothin'. Gettin' to be a nuisance. Hey, you fellers wouldn't go over theah and pick her up, would yuh?"

"Course we would, Bette," purred Hawkeye.

At Jocko Allcock's pad, Wooden Leg knocked on the door and yelled, "Okay, Alice, you been saved enough. Bette wants you to get back and take care of Big Dumpsmell."

The Reverend Mr. Rankin appeared, demanding, "What is the meaning of this. The young lady and I are in religious consultation."

"Zip up your fly and knock off that consultation crap. Fella like you shouldn't exercise too much on Sunday," Wooden Leg admonished him. "Now tell that broad to get out heah. Big Dumpsmell don't like to be kept waitin'."

Graveyard Alice flounced out, sort of. "Thanks, fellas," she said. "The jerk can't decide whether to pray or what. I been gettin' a complex. Guess I'd just as leave have Big Dumpsmell. In ninety seconds he goes home happy without no talk."

The Reverend Mr. Rankin took this all in. Hawkeye said later, "I couldn't help feeling sorry for the simple sonovabitch, so I didn't rub it in. I didn't even let him see me. Hope he can get his kicks out of his wife and *The Joy of Sex* for a while."

At Bette Bang Bang's, Juicy Larkin was timed in 58.5

152

seconds, which broke the house record for men over forty-five and gratified Graveyard Alice no end. She was spent after a busy Saturday night and an hour of religious consultation with the Reverend, who, she said, had studied *The Joy of Sex* as assiduously as he had the Bible.

And so it came to pass that with his physical ashes recently hauled, a cleanish if not immaculate body, cleanish if not stylish clothes, twenty bucks in his pocket and half a case of Gansett sloshing around in his pendulous belly, Juicy Larkin showed up Tuesday afternoon to be psychoanalyzed by Rex Eatapuss. He had been provided with a white coat, like the doctor he was impersonating, and Trapper John had wired him for sound, so that the analysis could be studied and enjoyed. Beyond this, Juicy had been given no specific instructions.

"Just lie down here on the couch, Doctor," purred Rex Eatapuss. "I'll sit here behind you. This will be very informal. What I'd like you to do is just relax. Let tension roll away. When you are relaxed, completely at ease, just tell me about yourself, anything. This is all in confidence. Nothing will go beyond this room."

There was silence for three minutes. The first sound that came, when the tape was played, was the sound of Juicy Larkin snoring.

Then, "Doctor, please wake up. Talk to me. Say something. Anything."

"That Alice be some finestkind diddlin', I'm here to tell yuh."

Rex: "I beg your pardon?"

Juicy: "Ain't you never tried her? Alice?"

Rex: "Perhaps we should try for a new start. Tell me, Doctor, what do you like to do, aside from your work?"

Juicy: "Hunt."

Rex, very hesitantly, uncertainly: "Oh, really? What do you hunt?"

Juicy: "Somethin you couldn't handle, I'll betcha."

And the audience, when it listened later, murmured in unison, "Oh, my Holy Jesus."

Rex: "Doctor, I don't think you are approaching this interview with the proper attitude. We do have a serious purpose, you know."

Juicy: "Sonovabitch, you don't mean it."

Rex: "I beg your pardon."

Juicy: "You mind if I have a bee-ah?"

Rex, confused: "I'm afraid I don't——"

Juicy: "Got one right heah in my pocket."

Juicy opened the beer, took a long pull, sighed and said, "Ain't that some good!"

Rex: "Dr. Maguire, this is a psychoanalysis, not a beer party."

Juicy: "Whadda you mean? I been wonderin'. You got a funny lookin' beard. Be you one of them quee-ahs? I tell you right now, you try somethin', I'll take aholt a you."

Rex, now clearly in retreat: "Please, Doctor, let's try to be impersonal. Can't you curb your obvious hostility? Can't you lie back with your beer and just tell me your thoughts?"

Juicy: "I'd like some."

Rex: "With all due respect, may I say that even for a surgeon, your general field of interest seems somewhat —ah—ah—carnal."

Juicy: "Ain't had a good carnival around heah for ten yeah. Jeezless cops run off the cooch shows."

Rex: "How would you know that, Doctor? Your record

indicates that you've just come from Iowa City."

Juicy: "I ain't no doctor. I'm a curator. You must be some mixed up. Queerest sonovabitch I ever see."

Rex: "The interview is over. But may I ask, of what are you the curator?"

Juicy: "Christly dump. That's what Hawkeye Pierce says I am. Curator."

Rex, screaming: "Get out of here, you animal!"

Juicy, vaguely sensing hostility in Rex Eatapuss, arose from the couch, decked the psychoanalyst with one roundhouse shot to the jaw and stalked out, dignified, in his white coat.

The next morning Hawkeye, just before he and Mary left for three weeks in sunny Portugal, called on me to say, "The Brain Trust and I have reached a decision. Rex and the Mental Health gang go. Gonzo. Goodbye. Upon my return, if not before, the wheels shall be set in motion."

9

SOCIAL SERVICE

I WASN'T too concerned with the psychoanalysis program, figuring that if half my staff would participate there'd be no problem with the federal subsidy. And indeed most of the staff cooperated. As conscientious physicians, they have a healthy intellectual interest in other specialties and felt that analysis might increase their understanding of themselves and their patients.

Naturally, inevitably, even before Hawkeye Pierce returned from Portugal, the small noisy minority was heard from. This happened even though I had given Dr. Ovari a list of people who were to be excused from the program. I suppose there was no way I could win. After considerable thought and with misgivings I put Dr. Al Black's name on the exempt list. Only later did it occur to me that all four of our black doctors were on this list.

Pierce arrived home from Portugal on the Sunday before Christmas. On Monday P.M. he and most of us attended Angelo's annual Christmas party at the Bay View. Hawkeye asked about the psychoanalysis business, and Wolfman Davis told him, "Everybody's doing it except you, Trapper, Boom-Boom, Duke and the four spooks."

"I think Dr. Albert Schwarzer, the Spade pediatrician who takes care of underprivileged honky kids, should get psyched," announced Hawkeye. "He may be strange."

"Out of the question," said Wolfman. "Everybody knows you can't psychoanalyze a spook, except of course, spook actors, who don't count."

Dr. Al Black is the only one of our black doctors who does not have a pro football background. He's just a little guy, and he may be almost as crazy as Hawkeye Pierce.

"I demand my rights," Al demanded, downing a generous portion of Angelo's booze. "I wanna get psychoanalyzed."

"I'll call the Mental Health Clinic and tell them we're bringing in an emergency case," said Hawkeye. "Get him some bananas."

Forthwith, the whole gang of crazies, eight or nine of them, poured out and into Spearchucker's station wagon carrying Al Black, who by now was munching on a banana and clutching a large bunch of them to his skinny bosom. At the Mental Health Clinic, minutes later, they bore him and the bananas directly to Dr. Ovari's office and deposited them all on the couch. Hawkeye and Spearchucker found Dr. Ovari and literally dragged him to the patient. Rex protested but was told, "Rex, this boy is in trouble. He's gone bananas. He needs psychoanalysis."

Again Rex protested, but Spearchucker said, "Now, Rex, I want you to take care of this young fella, or you and me going to have to have a little talk."

Hardly anyone argues with Spearchucker Jones, particularly if he mentions "a little talk," so Rex reluctantly began his interview, which, like Juicy Larkin's, was bugged.

Rex: "How do you feel, Doctor?"

Al Black: "Like I've eaten a whole bunch of bananas."

Rex: "Do bananas have some special significance to you?"

Al Black: "Come on, you old hunkie honkie, have a banana. Finestkind!"

Rex: "Thank you, no."

Al: "Man, do bananas have some special significance to you?"

Rex: "I'm conducting this examination, not you."

Al: "Can you sing 'The Winnipeg Whore'?"

Rex: "I'm afraid not."

Al: "I'll teach you: 'My first trip to the Bay of Fundy, first time on Canadian shores, there I met Mrs. Michael O'Finnegan, commonly known as the Winnipeg Whore.' Now you take the second verse, Rex. Fine tune, ain't it?"

Rex: "I'm sorry. I don't know the words to the second verse."

Al: "If you don't know the words to the second verse, how about showing me your——."

Just what Al wanted to see we'll never know because Rex interrupted quickly: "I'm afraid that your problem is beyond psychoanalysis. I must refer you to the psychiatrist, Dr. Davis."

" 'Then along that river bank a thousand miles, the tattoed cannibals danced in files.' Man, I gonna eat you, you hunkie honkie, but first I gotta get me a kettle and some Adolph's meat tenderizer. You stay right here, Rex. I'll be back in jig time."

Dr. Albert Schwarzer, the psychoanalysis over, returned to the Bay View where the tape was played for the edification of the assembled multitude, who cheered enthusiastically. By now the situation had progressed to where there was strong sentiment in favor of having a cookout with Rex Eatapuss as the cookee.

Saner minds prevailed as a few wives, hearing of trouble, came to rescue their loved ones and get them back on a proper pre-Christmas program.

I had believed, not just hoped, that once the holidays were over and the routine returned to normal, heat would be off the Mental Health Clinic. In fact, by early January I had nearly forgotten the trouble and crossed it off my worry list. Then Hawkeye dropped in late one afternoon and said, "Hook, Rex and the rest of the psychologists gotta go. We've had it with them. They got too much hair and too few brains."

"What do you mean?" I asked, not too brightly.

"I've had it. We've all had it. I take care of some grunt who shoots himself in the chest, Spearchucker's got the same deal in the head, or a broad with six kids and a drunk husband gets cancer of the boob, we inherit them forever. They ain't got enough to eat, they're nervous, they can't get a job, the old man beats 'em up—you name it. Who do they call? They call the guy who operated on them. Christ Jesus, they get a ticket for drunk driving they call the guy who operated on them. I, Trapper, all of us spend half our time running a social service agency. So along comes the Mental Health Clinic and a Social Service Department and a Department of Rehabilitation, bunch of dinks like Rex Eatapuss, long hairs in VW vans with Impeach Nixon and Recall Ford written on 'em, them dinks are gonna take care of the grunts, leave surgery to the surgeons, medicine to the internists, bring happiness to the unhappy. They probably got a payroll of a hundred and fifty big ones just for secretaries over there in that half mil building, and as far as anybody I know can figure out, all they do is have a daily ring dub and fill out a lotta forms. You write them a letter and tell them about somebody who needs help, they write you back the same letter and say they're gonna look into it. And two days later the patient's back in my office, somebody's office, saying they're nervous or the old man beat 'em up again. You ask 'em why don't they go to the Mental Health Clinic or Social Service, they say Mental Health had 'em fill out a form and if they got problems see their personal physician. Then you call one of the dumb bastards, they give you a lotta bull like somebody is gonna assess the home situation but they ain't got it cleared with the head misfit at the State House, or some ex-lush who's running this agency or that because he flunked out of life.

"My Holy Jumped Up Jesus! And you know, don't you, that's how the whole government runs at every level. A psychologist in Spruce Harbor is just a minor league version of a congressman in Washington. Give the dink the job, he figures he's got a mandate to malfease. He can get famous second-guessing Kissinger. But no way dinks like this ever gonna even try to do their job. And maybe they're right. They try, somebody shafts 'em. Still and all, this does nothing for the lame, the halt, the old, the deserving poor or the millions of just plain bums who, if you don't help them, are gonna make everything worse. Jesus Christ, it's enough to make you sick. Vermont got $900,000 to 'study medical needs in Vermont.' Now ain't that something? They'll hire twenty hairy incompetents who couldn't get from Montpelier to Burlington to 'make a study' and in three years the dough will be gone and not a jeezely cent spent on taking care of anyone. And the newspapers will give grunts like this three col-

160

umns a week telling how great they are. The guys taking care of the sick people, workin' like hell, doing most of what these jerks are supposed to be doing in addition to our own jobs, we're a bunch of predators on society because we can afford a country club."

"Does that conclude your speech?" I asked when he paused for a moment.

"Hell, no. Fifteen years ago, just for emphasis, we all took care of these people pretty well, for no dough and with considerable effort and with the help of a few fairly bright State types who'd do what the doctors told them. It wasn't perfect by a long shot, but believe me, I think it was better than it is now. We've had a proliferation of these hairy forty-hour-a-week amateurs who are accomplishing less than we did and costing five times as much. Meanwhile the busy doctors are still the backbone of the effort because most of us are nice to the losers, sympathize or try to help if only to get 'em the christ off our backs. And all they get from the hair is a date to come in and be told to keep a stiff upper lip. Jesus Christ, last week I had to call Joe Robbins and tell him to put furnace oil in some broad's house or I'd kick hell out of him, and he did it. The broad has cancer, no husband, three kids, no money—and those mental health social service losers couldn't do a thing for her. I could, so what the Christ *are they* for?"

"I heard about that. The Social Service people were working on it and they've made arrangements to take care of that the rest of the winter."

"Yeah, but by the time those creeps got around to it, that family would have had to get through two subzero nights with no heat."

161

"True," I had to agree, "but did you really accomplish anything by chasing that young social worker across the parking lot?"

"Yeah, I did. That was just after the broad called and told me she had no oil for her furnace and that jerk told her to fill out a form. I knew she couldn't fill out a form because she can't read or write and she's ashamed, but the dink doesn't know that. I happened to be in the hospital just as he was quitting for the day at four o'clock. I chased him out to his van with the Recall Ford sign on it. I had the freak so shook up he couldn't get that van movin' before I finished micturating in his gas tank. He didn't get too far once he got it started."

"So that's what happened. He was quite upset."

"Ain't that a pity? Pardon me if I don't choke up. You know these holier-than-thou eight-hours-a-day humanitarians are just a bunch of zips who couldn't get into medical school, don't you? So they take courses in psychology, learn five big words, grow some hair, find out where to buy cheap wine and tell each other they're better than surgeons who drive big cars and drink Chivas Regal."

"There's just one thing I'd like to say," I said.

"What's that?"

"No way you could beat hell out of Joe Robbins."

"Of course not, but you miss the point. One of these dinks calls Joe and gives him a lot of jazz about delivering oil, Joe's gonna wanta see the money, not a lotta forms, and he may decide to work the dink over just to keep in shape. When I call up and explain the situation, a guy like Joe says, 'Sure, Hawk, I'll keep her full the winter. Just don't tell nobody.' As a matter of fact, Joe keeps a few others full for nothin' because having to have anything to do with the dinks makes him nervous."

"You sound just like the medical profession from time immemorial," I suggested to my irate surgeon. "You're ticked off, the government's screwing everything up, but you guys aren't providing the answer either. You don't seriously suggest that, in the 1970's, we can take care of the poor, the handicapped, without help from Social Service and Mental Health facilities?"

"You're right. We haven't provided the answer, but we're gonna. Maybe our answer wouldn't swing in the city, but we're gonna upgrade the facilities around here."

"How?"

"You just relax, Hook, and enjoy it. Watch it evolve."

I waited and not much seemed to happen for weeks, except that early in January 1975 Wooden Leg Wilcox withdrew $100,000 from the hospital account and bought Chrysler stock. Two weeks later he sold it at a profit of $60,000 and replaced the hundred grand.

Although I kept my ears open and obliquely nudged Pierce when I had the chance, I heard nothing more except that, on February 26, Wooden Leg and Jocko Allcock departed for a week in Las Vegas. Ostensibly they were to visit Leg's sister and her rich husband, Benny Aaron. This meshed with rumors that Leg and Jocko, gamblers by profession, had been going here and there to study the game of baccarat. By that I mean, of course, they were learning how to emerge triumphantly by cheating.

March came in like a lion, accompanied by the announcement that Miss Priscilla Poissonier, B.A., M.S., had joined the Spruce Harbor Mental Health Center as a psychiatric social worker. Specifically, Uncle was pop-

163

ping for for twelve G's a year for Priscilla to be a rape counselor.

If Blue Shield had announced a doubling of or halving of surgical fees, my surgical staff would have reacted a little, or not at all. But they thought a rape counselor was the greatest thing since the wheel. Masochistically I went to the coffee shop, always a beehive of gossip, to hear the reactions, which were predictable.

"Just what we need," said Hawkeye. "I been worried about how to go about it."

"About what?" Duke asked.

"Rapin' some broad."

"You must be gettin' desperate," thought Trapper.

"Not really. It's just that I'm fifty years old now, never raped anybody. I figure time's passing me by. I don't do it soon, may never get around to it."

"Well, now," said Spearchucker, "maybe we oughta ask this young lady in for a cuppa coffee and some counseling. I'll see if I can dig her up."

"She's right over there with Dr. Ovari," the waitress told them. The waitresses always listen to the surgeons.

Spearchucker introduced himself and invited her to join their table. "We understand you graduated summa cum laude from rape school and we have a small problem," he explained. "I'd like you to meet Dr. Pierce."

"Oh, how do you do, Dr. Pierce. I've heard so much about you," Priscilla exclaimed.

"Perhaps you could help Dr. Pierce," said Trapper. "He's planning to rape someone but has no experience."

"Always had to beat it off with a club," Hawkeye told her modestly. "No experience at all."

"I'm afraid I don't understand."

"Well, just what does your counseling service provide?

Like, who selects the victim, you or me? Like do I whack her around a little first, I mean, honey, supposin' I was to take a liking to you, would I wait for you in your apartment or grab you on the way home or——"

Miss Poissonier gave a little squeal and departed abruptly.

"We gotta help that girl out," said Chucker. "Unless we do, she won't have work and our taxpayers' money will be wasted. As far as I know, we don't have more'n two or three rapes a year."

Duke mulled this and asked, rather fearfully, "What measures do you contemplate, Chucker?"

"Well, now, I've had this hankerin' for Lucinda McIntyre——"

"Won't work," Trapper objected.

"Now, why not, Honkie? You sayin' I ain't——"

"All I'm sayin' is no way you could rape her. She'd think bedding a nigger was part of women's lib. In fact, I figured you and she'd already——"

"Now wait a damned——"

"Knock it off, you guys," Hawkeye ordered. "Surely men as resourceful as we can fulfill this young lovely's needs without interfamilial sexual coercion."

"What's that mean?"

"Rapin' each other's wives."

"What measures do *you* recommend?"

"I say we keep the dolly busy interviewing rape victims."

"Brilliant," agreed Duke. "Who's gonna be the rapers and who's gonna be the rapees? Hope we can get this settled before we have to go back to the O.R."

"Why, the rapees can be the broads from Bette Bang Bang's. And the rapers could be, well, almost anyone

165

who has now, or in the past, fallen from favor, or whatever."

"Goofus MacDuff's been actin' right stemmy lately," Dr. Jones observed.

"Don't be foolish," said Duke. "He couldn't get it up. Let's go. They must be ready for us by now."

At eleven o'clock that night the Emergency Room called to tell me that a rape case had been brought in. The nurse in charge seemed to feel that the case had certain curious aspects since the victim was Graveyard Alice. Priscilla Poissonier was already there when I arrived, in camera with Alice, assuring her that all would be well.

Priscilla Poissonier, fresh from rape school, was gently, sympathetically questioning Alice, who sobbed uncontrollably, interspersing the sobs with "that old sonovabitch."

"Don't be afraid, Alice," purred Priscilla. "The law will protect you. If you'll just tell me who it was, I promise you this will never happen to anyone else."

" 'Twas Doggy done it," she blurted out.

At Miss Poissonier's insistence, Dr. Doggy Moore was arrested an hour later as he left the delivery room. Smiling with modest pride, he was taken downtown, booked and released on ten thousand dollars bail. When asked about this the next day by concerned citizens, Dr. Moore said, "My lawyer has told me not to discuss the case, but I can say this much: Ain't no doubt about it. I done it."

On the afternoon after the rape, Irene (Bull) Benson, coach of Spruce Harbor High's girls' basketball team, chairman of SHARC (Spruce Harbor Anti-Rape Committee), led twenty of her minions in a loud demonstration outside the courthouse to protest Dr. Moore's freedom on bail. And the next day, the protest having been mostly ignored, Bull led her group right up to the hospital and camped in the coffee shop, apparently hoping to picket Doggy. He was quite happy. "Good morning to you, ladies," he greeted them. "Any of you girls want some action, I'll be waiting outside in my station wagon."

SHARC gasped, like all in one breath. Trapper John called Bull aside and said, "Bull, get this passel of wool outa here or we gonna have Spearchucker knock you off one by one right here on the counter."

Bull hesitated. "Okay, Chucker, we'll hold her down," said Trapper. "You can start reeling it out."

Bull screamed and SHARC retreated, a defeated rag-tag mob. Regrouping outside, SHARC stormed the office of the Spruce Harbor *Gazette*, where Bull hysterically told of attempted mass rape of SHARC by the surgical staff of Spruce Harbor Medical Center. This kept things stirred up, but SHARC really was a toothless organization and public interest lagged in a matter of days. In fact, the most exciting event of the following week was the elimination of Bull Benson's team from the Class B Girls' Basketball Tournament.

One afternoon well into March I had a phone call about three o'clock. My secretary told me that I was to have the pleasure of speaking to the Stoned Eagle, Mr. Wrong Way Napolitano.

"Big jeezely airplane, like some kinda Army cargo plane, out here," said Wrong Way. "Some general claims he knows you, wants somebody to come get the tents. Better get out here. Christly general's into my booze."

"What's his name?"

There was a lull while, in the background, I heard, "General, whatcha say yer name was?"

"Blake, Henry, Major General Army Medical Corps. Tell Hook or Hawkeye or somebody, get them out here."

This came as a slight surprise. Henry Blake, former C.O. of the 4077th MASH, had stayed in the Army and, as suggested by his rank, prospered in a pentagonal way. He may be our nation's premier latrine officer or the head Army clap doctor. Who knows? You ask him, the answer is so long you forget the question. Fact is, here he was at Spruce Harbor International with a planeful of tents and I didn't know why.

I was pretty sure Pierce knew, so I called his office. His secretary, Alice D'Angelo, told me he couldn't be disturbed.

"This is important," I protested. "Is he with a patient?"

"No, he's devoting the remainder of the day to two major efforts. I have the list right here. When I read it to you, I'm sure you'll understand why he cannot be disturbed."

She read: "I am not to be disturbed for the following reasons: (1) I want to listen to Wolf Creek Pass by C. W. McCall, probably the greatest musical triumph of the century, and I can't listen at home because the house apes won't shut up long enough, and (2) I must observe a half hour of silent mourning for Chief Jay Strongbow whose feathered headdress was torn to shreds by Gorilla Monsoon."

Alice concluded, "Surely now you understand why he cannot be disturbed."

"I'll be right down. He's gonna get disturbed."

I barged into Hawkeye's office in time to hear the stirring end of Wolf Creek Pass in which a runaway truck full of chickens takes out a feed store at the bottom of the Great Divide.

"Tremendous," Hawkeye exclaimed. "What's up, administrative type who obviously has no respect for my privacy, to say zip of the feathered headdress handed down through eight generations to Chief Jay Strongbow."

"Having you put away is on my list, but the immediate problem is that Henry Blake is at the airport with a bunch of tents."

"Finestkind. Things working out okay. Just heard from our old friend Benny Aaron. Wooden Leg and Jocko won two hundred big ones at baccarat out in Vegas. Benny's having them flown home if his Lear jet can evade about twenty guinea fighter planes. Seems the folks running the game questioned our men's honesty. Let's go out and meet Henry."

I got no more out of him and, since he was driving, there was little opportunity for talk. When riding with Pierce, particularly on ice and snow, one tends to contemplate one's past and reevaluate one's future, if any. We skidded into the parking area behind the home office of the Spruce Harbor & Inter-Island Air Service. Major General Henry Blake, twenty pounds heavier than Korea and holding, came out to greet us.

"How's your GI ass, Henry?" Pierce asked.

"Great. Hi, Hook. Where you guys want these tents?"

"I don't know anything about the tents," I said, "and no one will tell me."

"For chrissake, Hook," Pierce explained, "the tents are the new nut and social service clinic. We gonna run Eatapuss and his crowd outa business. Whadda we owe you for the tents, Henry? Hey, did you bring those space heater rigs we asked for?"

"Yeah, everything. You don't owe me a cent. Government's glad to get rid of the stuff. Transportation's free, too. Training flight."

"Finestkind," said Hawk. "Wonder how we're gonna get all that stuff moved and set up."

"Christly governor," muttered Wrong Way Napolitano, who, until now, had just been nursing a highball because he might have to fly at any time.

We all paused to ponder his straightforward lucid statement. "You are trying to tell us something, Great Stoned Eagle," said Hawkeye, "but so far, just what eludes me."

"Call Crazy Horse, tell him get National Guard transport the stuff, set it up. Trainin' exercise."

"Wrong Way, you do occasionally think. However, I never make phone calls. You call him. I'll talk to him." (The story of Crazy Horse Weinstein's dramatic triumph in the election of November 1974 will be told in a forthcoming volume.)

Wrong Way and the General and all of us were quite a bit further into the office booze when the governor finally answered.

"Hi, Horse," Hawk greeted him. "The grunts in the legislature say you're insensitive to the needs of the people. I hear the wool libbers are gonna get you, the Indians are gonna scalp you and you been excommunicated by B'nai B'rith for making some camel driver attorney general. Aside from these minor tribulations, I trust all is well?"

I don't know the governor's precise response, but Dr. Pierce's reaction gives a hint. "Do not speak to one of your loyal supporters in such peremptory terms, particularly when I am trying to do you a favor. Here's the deal, Horse. We got some old Army hospital tents, space heaters, other stuff. We want you to get out the Guard, set it all up. Then we gonna run a self-supporting, efficient Mental Health, Psychiatric and Social Service Center. Gonna save State of Maine hundreds of thousands of dollars. Leg and Jocko raised quarter mil gonna pay off government for Mental Health Clinic we got now, turn it into new fish market and finestkind seafood restaurant on the whole coast, maybe even Last Supper Specials, two lobsters for a fin the night before surgery. Gonna make medical history, deliver super service to the unhappy and the screwed up at fraction of present cost. And here's the clincher, Crazy Horse. We gonna give *you* the credit."

Again, the governor's response, while unheard, became quite clear when Hawkeye said, "May Arafat become your Prime Minister and the palefaces rape your women. Okay, just send the Guard. We won't give you credit for it."

"That takes care of that," said Hawk, putting down the phone. "Henry, you're staying at Trapper John's house, but first we will take you to the Bay View for a couple pops and introduce you to the local citizenry."

The subsequent events were quite upsetting to me then, although now that time has passed and my troops have done nothing too crazy for several months, I am finally able to recall that period without needing a tranquilizer. General Blake, although we'd all seen him at various meetings and in Washington in the twenty-two years since we left Korea, had never before visited Spruce Harbor. The moment we entered the Bay View,

171

I realized that preparations had been made in his honor. Sitting at the bar, dressed like a black-headed grosbeak, was Halfaman Timberlake. Next to Halfaman, sort of draped over another bar stool, was Halfaman's shackmate and constant companion of three years, Twiceabear. This creature is a two-hundred-pound, overfed, docile, toothless and clawless (courtesy local surgeon) brown Maine bear that Halfaman rescued as a cub and has nurtured ever since. Twiceabear was eating from a large bowl of spaghetti.

Hawkeye made the introductions. "Angelo," he said, "this general was my C.O. in Korea. Make him a nice martini. Henry, meet the guinea runs the joint, Angelo."

"You only had them a little while, General. I've had them eighteen years. How you think I feel?"

"You have my deepest sympathy, Angelo," the General assured him, all the time peeking at Halfaman and Twiceabear out of the corner of an eye.

"And now, Henry," said Pierce, "I want you to meet the Director of the Maine Audubon Society and Vice President of our hospital's Board of Trustees, Professor Timberlake."

General Blake hesitated momentarily before extending a hand of greeting to Professor Timberlake, who, shaking the hand energetically, said, "Your daughter sleeps with snakes. This here's my friend, Twiceabear."

Henry Blake, as in the dim past, sort of gulped like a frog and sipped his martini. "It's all coming back to me," he said. "I wonder what will happen next?"

"Relax, Henry," counseled Hawkeye. "You know these professors. All kinda strange. Let's sit down. Trapper, Duke, Chucker, they'll be here soon."

The door opened and, lo and behold, there stood Priscilla Poissonier and Edie with the Great Big Pair and Double Bubble Harkness, the assistant chief of police. "That's the one in the Army suit," proclaimed Edie. "He done raped me."

Double Bubble Harkness, who is fat in both the chest and the belly and has two blue bubbles on his car, has been on a certain list of Hawkeye's because of alleged traffic violations. Double Bubble approached General Blake and said, "You are under arrest for rape, you."

"Excuse me, Double Bubble," said Hawkeye, "with all due respect to the low IQ which is part of your job description, has it occurred to you that before arresting a Major General in the Army Medical Corps for rape, you should do a little basic investigation?"

"The woman says the guy done it, Doctor. I know what you think of me, but I got no choice."

"You got no choice, Double Bubble, because you are a moron. Why don't you ask Wrong Way, me and Hooker to account for the General's time since he landed in Spruce Harbor at three o'clock?"

"Tain't up to me. I'm just answerin' a complaint."

Spearchucker Jones arrived just in time to catch this bit. Dr. Jones has a certain prestige, power, respect, whatever, which my other nuts don't. He took over. He said, "Double Bubble, go home, take the whore and the little social worker with you and try not to bother the upper classes again today."

"Okay, gentlemen," Spearchucker said then. "I think somebody's carried this too far. General Blake is giving us our new clinic, he took care of us in Korea, he comes to see us, somebody sets him up for rape. Man, somebody's got a twisted mind."

"It's my fault," said Trapper. "All I did was call the

173

whorehouse, say Henry might want to get laid, have Edie on call. Bette Bang Bang got it all screwed up, thought it was another rape job. I shoulda known better."

"Sure," Hawkeye said with understanding, "you were trying to do the right thing. We'll forgive you, won't we, Henry?"

"That looked like pretty good stuff," said General Blake. "Maybe——"

"Later, Henry. We'll have a couple drinks and then go to Thief Island for our joyous reunion."

In the confusion following the disappearance of Double Bubble, Priscilla Poissonier and Edie with the Great Big Pair, Halfaman and Twiceabear stealthily crept away. They had been given a very responsible and demanding assignment by Trapper John and Jocko Allcock. And, two martinis later, Major General Blake, accompanied by his loyal ex-staff, departed for Thief Island, the home of Dr. and Mrs. John Francis Xavier McIntyre.

By midevening the festive group, including wives, was sitting around the great fireplace sipping brandy and reminiscing when the sound of a boat was heard. Ere long we were joined by Professor Timberlake of the Audubon Society, his faithful companion Twiceabear, and Mr. Jocko Allcock.

"The Professor and me can help ourselves, Lucinda," Jocko told the hostess, "but Twiceabear needs a large bowl of porridge. He's some used up."

Just what Lucinda McIntyre planned to do about the porridge we'll never know because the quiet of the night was shattered by the siren on the Spruce Harbor Police boat, which splashed to an earsplitting stop at Trapper's wharf. Out jumped Double Bubble Harkness, Priscilla

174

Poissonier and Edie with the Great Big Pair, who ran right into the house without so much as a knock on the door. "That's him," screeched Edie, pointing at Twiceabear, "the big dude in the fur coat."

"I swear to Christ," exclaimed Hawkeye, "I can't believe it." Crossing the room quickly, he put his arm around the accused and pleaded, "Say it ain't so, Twiceabear."

"Arrest that dude," Priscilla Poissonier exhorted Double Bubble.

"That bear like to eat me," mumbled the people's champion.

"You gonna take him in, you gotta read him his rights," Spearchucker warned. "And you do have a reading problem, don't you Bubble?"

"Huh."

"Let him stay free on his own recognizance, Bubble," Duke suggested. "Unless yuh-all wanta tangle with a bear. Just have the judge let him know when to show up for the trial."

"I guess that'll be okay."

Priscilla Poissonier was horrified. "SHARC shall hear of this," she screamed in indignation.

"Honey," Hawkeye said sweetly, "tell SHARC all about it, but we're having a quiet little reunion here. You get that bunch of dykes over here tonight, our friendly game might get rough. Now you go home and lock your doors and don't let any bears in."

General Blake flew back to Washington the next day, and two new psychiatrists recruited by Wolfman Davis arrived in Spruce Harbor. No one doubted that the newcomers were psychiatrists because, like Wolfman, they had black beards. I was inclined to agree with Dr. Pierce who said, "Them three together look like the Olympic anarchy squad."

Within a week many truckfuls of gravel had been deposited on the site of the new clinic to serve as the floor, the tents had been erected and the heaters installed. Wolfman moved in with his crew, three psychiatrists, six secretaries, three social workers and three psychologists who had not voted for McGovern in 1972. Wooden Leg Wilcox explained to the leftover psychologists that their best bet was to leave town, but if they wanted to they could pick shrimp for him till the new restaurant opened and then they could work as waiters because, as a concession to the times, he hoped to create a "slightly fag atmosphere."

After two weeks the superiority of the new Finestkind Clinic for the confused and the Downtrodden (as it was called by the surgeons) over its predecessor became obvious. The volume had already increased slightly and the efficiency tripled. I did get a larger number of phone calls from State House types complaining of certain arbitrary decisions made by the new clinic. Usually I was able to smooth the waters by asking whether the costs were climbing or subsiding. Since they were subsiding, and since public officials are sensitive to public reaction, just asking the question usually sufficed. When it didn't, I usually suggested that they present their complaints to Governor Weinstein. I did this with the knowledge that, after early doubt, Crazy Horse had recognized the value of the new clinic and blessed it.

Courts anywhere, and grand juries, work in peculiar ways. This is a result of a variety of factors, the basic factor being that the people who manage these situations are, to quote Dr. Pierce, "Just plain dumb." Thus

176

it was that in early April the Spruce Harbor *Gazette* announced triumphantly: "Dr. Moore and T. Timberlake Indicted for Rape."

I was, as they say, beside myself, whatever that means. I had, reasonably, assumed that this charade would be concluded long before it reached a courtroom. The idea of a seventy-seven-year-old physician and a bear being prosecuted for raping two prostitutes was preposterous. Once I got out from beside myself, I got good and mad. I have enough troubles without one of my staff being tried for rape. Pierce was the first of the conspirators I could find, and I demanded an explanation.

"Nothing to explain. They were both arrested, as you know. Twiceabear got on the docket as T. Timberlake. It was just due process of law. Nobody did a thing, Hook. Of course, maybe we could have, but we've been dying of curiosity to see how far these numbies will carry it before the absurdity becomes obvious even to them."

"Yeah, but for chrissake, two whores——"

"Hold up," he interrupted. "Remember we got this young guy for D.A. You know the young lawyers like to be D.A. so they can get a reputation. Then they go into practice and use what they've learned putting the grunts in jail to keep the grunts out of jail. Most lawyers are basically unendowed with smarts. About the only difference between them and the grunts is they can read and write a little. This new D.A., I've encountered him at Industrial Accident hearings. He doesn't know the difference between a chiropractor and a board certified orthopod. And in this case, he doesn't know that Sue Ellen Crabtree and Rosemary Maginnis are Graveyard Alice and Edie with the Great Big Pair. He ain't asked, so nobody's told him. Also, Bull Benson and SHARC are on his back. Bull thinks she's gonna get enough mileage out of this case to run for the legislature. And the D.A., he figures if he can put away the area's most respected physician, he can run for Congress, the ultimate goal of all unsuccessful lawyers."

"Yeah, but even Georgie Howell, he's the D.A., isn't that dumb. He must know who these broads are!"

"Well, you gotta remember, the whorehouse set is not dominant in this community. What the hell, you expect Stiff Standing Hooper, other guys who occasionally tap a strange one, are gonna go to the D.A. and say, 'Hey, boy, that Sue Ellen is a whore. I should know.'? What's more, Jocko's moved them both into his pad and spread it around they give dancing lessons."

"But they're not really going to testify?"

"Not really. They'll show up for the trial, but I doubt like hell if they'll have to testify. Jim Carr's gonna be the judge."

"So what?"

"Well, hell, you know Jim. He's one of three or four in the state got any brains. Most of the judges are just gomers can't hack private practice, kiss enough to get a permanent job for less than my income tax. Christ, I knew two of them went to Androscoggin. I had to teach the dumb bastards to spell."

"What makes you think you succeeded?" I asked.

"I don't think I did."

"But what's your admiration for the legal profession got to do with Judge Carr and this case?"

"Jesus, Hook, you know Jim. His wife died what, three or four years ago. He's been bangin' that Molly a little but he's gotta be discreet. Molly ain't too available, guy's gotta get some. Jocko fixes him up at his pad now and

178

then. Jim knows all the girls. In fact, the only reason, probably, the trial hasn't been called off is Jim's been down on Treasure Cay the last month, gonna come into this kinda cold."

Indeed, this was one of the shortest trials in history. The defendants were there, represented by Jim Holden. SHARC, mostly Bull Benson, was there. Graveyard Alice and Edie with the Great Big Pair were there. Judge Carr had no more than convened the court than Doggy Moore got up and said, "I done it, Judge. I'm guilty as hell."

Judge Carr looked at Doggy, at Twiceabear, clad in a white shirt with buttondown collar and a blue-and-red striped tie. He conferred with a bailiff who told him that Alice and Edie were the complaining parties. He banged his gavel and growled, "Case dismissed." Summoning the D.A., he said, "See me in my chambers, young man." Summoning the bailiff again, he ordered, "Joe, get that bear out of my courtroom."

The Finestkind Seafood Restaurant (Last Supper Specials, $5) opened for business on June 1, 1975. The manager and genial host, Dr. Ferenc Ovari, was pictured in multiple TV ads prior to the grand opening. His grand manner, his mid-European (Scranton?) accent, were natural assets which, by mid-July, had attracted the summer complaints in droves.

"Rex is a born thief and a con man to boot," explained Wooden Leg. "But how much can a guy steal runnin' a Mental Health Clinic in Spruce Harbor, Maine? Runnin' a restaurant, we can use his natural skills."